SECOND TIME AROUND

SECOND TIME AROUND

Vanessa Graham

CHIVERS
THORNDIKE

This large print book is published by BBC Audiobooks Ltd, Bath, England and by Thorndike Press, Waterville, Maine, USA.

Published in 2003 in the U.K. by arrangement with the author.

Published in 2003 in the U.S. by arrangement with Juliet Burton Literary Agency.

U.K. Hardcover   ISBN 0–7540–7314–9   (Chivers Large Print)
U.K. Softcover   ISBN 0–7540–7315–7   (Camden Large Print)
U.S. Softcover   ISBN 0–7862–5670–2   (General Series)

The text of this Large Print edition is unabridged.
Other aspects of the book may vary from the original edition.

Set in 16 pt. New Times Roman.

Printed in Great Britain on acid-free paper.

British Library Cataloguing in Publication Data available

Library of Congress Cataloging-in-Publication Data

Graham, Vanessa.
    Second time around / Vanessa Graham.
      p.   cm.
    ISBN 0–7862–5670–2 (lg. print : sc : alk. paper)
    1. Remarried people—Fiction. 2. Large type books. I. Title.
PR6056.R286S47 2003
823'.914—dc21   2003053312

CHAPTER ONE

I glanced at my watch and then, impatiently, along the hallway to the swing doors. It always irritated me when David kept me waiting. The film started at seven-thirty and unless he was quick, we shouldn't have time for a meal beforehand: which meant another late night. Not a good policy midweek, with the pressure that was on at the office at the moment.

The doors started to revolve again, and a man came quickly into the hall. It wasn't David, and I was about to look away when something about the set of his shoulders and his purposeful stride struck a chord inside me and started a discordant jangling.

As though mesmerized I rose slowly to my feet, staring at him as he came towards me—at the rather hard face with the firm chin and disillusioned eyes. My heart gave a little jerk and as he drew level I said tentatively, as much to myself as to him, 'Simon?'

He stopped abruptly, his head turned and for a moment his eyes raked my face. Then slow-dawning recognition flickered.

'Good Lord, it's not—?'

'Cherry,' I supplied shakily. 'Cherry Lester.'

'Little Cherry—ye gods! What are you doing so far from home?'

'I live in London now.'

1

'Do you indeed? Well, well! I'd never have recognized you. How long has it been?'

'About six years, I suppose. I—thought you were in Africa?'

'Got back last month. What a coincidence, though, meeting you like this. Come and have a drink and tell me all the news.'

'I'd love to but I'm afraid I can't. I'm—meeting someone.' And over his shoulder at last I saw David emerge from the maw of the swing doors—just when I least wanted him.

'Of course—stupid of me. You'd hardly have been here if you weren't.'

David came up to us and I managed the introductions a little stumblingly.

'Perhaps we could make it another evening,' Simon said easily. 'Give me your phone number and I'll ring you.'

Out of the corner of my eye I saw that David had the gall to look at his watch. I gave Simon my number, but without hope. It was a graceful let-out but I doubted that he had any real intention of phoning. After all, what was the point?

David took my arm firmly and we were out on the pavement at the mercy of the biting wind. 'I'm surprised you fell for that line,' he said sullenly. '"Give me your phone number" indeed!'

'Don't be silly, David. He's an old friend of the family. Actually, he was married to my cousin.'

2

'Was?'

'Yes, they were divorced a couple of years ago. Anyway, if you hadn't been late I'd never have met him.'

'Okay, okay, I couldn't help it. Let's nip into the Chicken Inn—it's all we have time for now.'

I sighed. It was always the same with David—rush, rush—abandoned plans and hasty improvisations. Simon, after all these years! He hadn't really changed: older, of course, and gorgeously tanned from his years in Africa, but still the same self-assured Simon. A thousand memories jostled for position in my head, but David was demanding my attention.

'Come on, Cherry, we haven't time to dawdle. The film starts in half an hour.'

Obediently I hurried through the meal, trying to anchor my racing thoughts. Perhaps he had remarried. Mother had mentioned in one of her letters that Cathy had a new admirer. I'd wondered fleetingly how she could be interested in anyone else after being married to Simon for eight years.

'Cherry!'

'Sorry.' I pushed the last of the food to the side of my plate. My appetite seemed to have disappeared anyway. We were out on the street again, wet now with an icy, drizzling rain, and dark in the early spring dusk. Oh, why couldn't David have been later still, or Simon earlier? Then he might have made a definite arrangement, instead of a vague promise to phone.

I pulled myself up sharply. Simon Slade was taboo. He always had been. Cathy's husband. Unwillingly my mind flickered to my cousin, with her pale hair and large appealing eyes: a helpless appearance which concealed a will of iron, as I had learned in my youth.

The film was, as usual, complicated and involved, and my eyes ached from trying to decipher the subtitles. The choice of it had been David's, of course. He considered I should be *au fait* with all the latest foreign films. But lately they'd seemed very much the same, and I had been hard put to it to display any intelligent interest. I realized belatedly that he hadn't taken my hand as he usually did. He probably still hadn't forgiven me for Simon. I gave up all pretence of concentrating on the film and, with a wave of relief, released the floodgates and let the memories come.

It all began with Cathy, of course. Her father, Mother's elder brother, had been killed in a car crash three months before she was born. During our childhood, she and Aunt Beth often came to stay with us, but as she was six years older than I we had never played well together. I used to trail around after her, getting in the way, lost in admiration and envy when she started to wear high heels and powder her nose. Then, when she was barely eighteen, she met Simon. From my first sight

4

of him, I'd suffered from a severe bout of hero-worship. Simon was to me what pop singers and TV stars were to my friends— someone to dream about, but completely out of reach. And they certainly made a striking couple, Cathy with her long fair hair and Simon so tall and dashing. And the look in his eyes when they rested on her sent little shivers down my back.

I was their bridesmaid and the occasion proved a landmark in a rather uneventful childhood, so that for years afterwards I dated things as having happened either before or after the wedding. Simon and Cathy moved to Surrey and gradually faded into the background of my mind—which became involved with a new school, exams, hockey matches. Their first child, James, was born a year later, and then Paul. Cathy wrote, of course, and Aunt Beth still came to stay, but gradually I began to be aware that things were not quite right. I caught odd snatches of conversations which were broken off when I came into the room. There were long phone calls from Aunt Beth, which Mother took privately on the upstairs extension. Once I heard my father say, 'Of course I was never happy about it, but you women wouldn't listen. He was altogether too fond of his own way.'

'That's not fair!' I broke in hotly. 'Cathy's the stubborn one!'

They stared at me in surprise and Mother

said sharply, 'Don't speak to your father like that, Cherry, and don't interfere in what is none of your business.'

I learned my lesson, but I had declared my allegiance without even considering it, and from time to time I thought about them both and wondered if they were happy. And later, as the boys from the tennis club started to call round, I unconsciously compared them, always to their disadvantage, with Simon Slade.

Until this evening, I had only seen him once more. He and Cathy came up north to show us the new baby—a girl at last. It was just before my sixteenth birthday and I was all legs and freckles. Cathy seemed smaller—no doubt because I myself had grown—and even paler than before, and there was a tight note in her voice when she spoke to Simon. He himself was tense and restless, unable to keep still for more than a few minutes at a time, and his eyes were brooding and unhappy. I startled myself with a sudden longing to take his hand and comfort him, and at the temerity of the thought my face had flamed and I'd had to turn hastily away. Remembering the incident now, my cheeks were hot again.

'I said,' remarked David in a raised voice, 'are you enjoying it?'

I started guiltily, wrenching my mind back to the present. 'Oh—yes, thanks.'

'Well, I'm still not clear who that fellow was, but I must say I don't care for the effect he's had on you. I might as well not be here, for all the notice you've taken of me this evening.'

'Oh David, I'm sorry,' I said contritely. 'It's just that it was rather a shock, coming on someone out of the past like that.'

'But not your past, surely?'

'My very tender youth!' I said with a smile, and he was satisfied.

It was eleven when I let myself into the flat, and Sue had just made the cocoa. 'Hello, you're early! We weren't expecting you for another hour.'

'What was the film like?' asked Lucy from under a curtain of hair that was drying in front of the gas fire.

'Much the same as usual.' I found myself a mug and held it out to Sue.

'You're somewhat flushed tonight,' she remarked astutely. 'Don't tell me David's making some headway at last!'

I laughed a little self-consciously. 'No, as a matter of fact I bumped into someone else while I was waiting for him. Someone I was madly in love with at the age of twelve!'

'Precocious little beast!' Lucy sat up, tossing back her mane of hair. 'Come on then, tell us more. Who was this dream boat?'

'It wouldn't convey anything to you, but he married my cousin.'

'The one who's divorced?'

'The same.'

'Ho, ho!' said Lucy, reaching up for her

cocoa. 'Re-enter hero, no longer out of reach!'

'Don't be ridiculous,' I said sharply.

She raised her eyebrows. 'Beg pardon, I'm sure!'

'Sorry. It was just—well, it shook me rather —seeing him, that's all.'

'Apparently,' said Sue drily. 'What happened? Are you going to see him again?'

'David arrived before anything was fixed. He did say he'd phone but he probably won't.'

'He might, though,' said Lucy thoughtfully, 'for news of his ex-wife.'

'Thanks for nothing.'

'Goodness, Cherry, I've never known you so touchy! Have you still got a thing about him?'

I gazed reflectively into the fire. 'To be honest, I don't know. If they'd gone on living near us and we'd seen a lot of them, no doubt the glamour would have worn off. But since they didn't, I never had a chance to grow out of it. He's probably been at the back of my mind ever since, as a kind of—blueprint. All of which,' I added, standing up suddenly, 'is extremely foolish, since my parents would have a fit if I so much as had a drink with him.'

I set the empty mug down on the mantelpiece with suppressed violence, aware of the exchanged glances behind my back.

'I'm going to bed,' I said.

The next ten days stretched bleakly into eternity. At the office I struggled to keep my mind on the job, but from the moment I entered the flat in the evening until the moment I got into bed, I was poised to answer the telephone. And of course it rang frequently—Tim, for Lucy; Steven, for Sue; David, for me. And each time it rang, I thought of the song, *Let it please be him*. And, as in the song, it never was.

At the end of two weeks I'd had enough. I took myself firmly in hand, ran through all the reasons why he would never phone, and why it was better that he shouldn't, and decided to close my mind to him once and for all. And that evening he phoned.

'Cherry?' Despite my resolve, I had flown to answer it. And at the sound of his voice at last, my knees gave way and I sat down suddenly. 'That you, Cherry?'

'Yes.'

'Simon here. Sorry not to have rung before but I mislaid your number. Still, all's well that ends well. I was wondering if you'd like to come out for a meal one evening?'

The arrangements were made and I carefully replaced the receiver. Lucy said softly, 'Hold on, Cherry. You're riding for a fall.'

'Agreed. "And all the king's horses and all the king's men—"'

'Then why risk it? You said your parents wouldn't approve.'

'I'm old enough to make my own decisions now,' I answered, with more assurance than I felt. But the next evening, as I sat across the table from Simon, I thought ruefully how unnecessary had been her warnings and how futile my own tenuous dreams over the last two weeks—for there was no hint of romance about Simon. In fact his manner, pleasant, relaxed and slightly teasing, was that of an older brother making the best of an evening in the company of his young sister. Yet what had I expected, I demanded savagely of myself: hearts and flowers? Two weeks ago, it had taken him all this time to recognize me. No doubt Lucy had been right after all and he simply wanted news of Cathy. As though to underline the bitterness of my conclusion, he handed the menu back to the waiter and said easily,

'Now, tell me all the news. How's the family? Your father still at the same bank?'

'Yes,' I answered brightly. 'He'll be there until he retires now.' Hands clenched in my lap, I waited, determined to volunteer nothing. He drew on his cigarette, put his head back and blew the smoke gently towards the ceiling. 'And Cathy?' he asked casually. 'How is she these days?'

If he wasn't embarrassed, I didn't see why I should be. I strove to keep my voice as offhand as his, 'I haven't seen her for a while, but I believe she's very well.'

'And the children?' A little muscle in his jaw let him down. Not quite so casual after all.

'I'm sorry, I really haven't any news of them. I've been down here for over a year now, and the last few times I've been home I didn't see them.'

'No. I see.' His eyes were still on the smoke. Perhaps he was reflecting that he was getting small return for the price of a meal. I moistened my lips.

'You haven't seen them yourself, then?'

'Not yet, no. Since I returned from Africa last month I've been desperately busy, and I don't particularly want to have to go up there and beard the lion—or lioness—in its den. It's a question really of arranging for them to come down here and see me. After all, I'm allowed what is quaintly called "reasonable access."'

At last his eyes came down to mine, and they were faintly embarrassed. 'I probably shouldn't be speaking to you like this; it puts you in a difficult position. I'm sorry.'

'It's all right,' I said inadequately. I could hardly tell him that I'd always been on his side. We were silent while the waiter brought the first course and laid it in front of us. I glanced round the restaurant, enjoying the unostentatious luxury. Very different from the meals I shared with David.

'Now, let's talk of more pleasant things. How long did you say you've been in the Big City?'

'About eighteen months.'

11

'And I suppose life is one long social round, with plenty of men at your feet? What it is to be young!'

My eyes flew to his face and he laughed. 'Come on now, you can tell Uncle! How many hearts have you broken? That young man the other evening seemed rather possessive, I thought.' He waited, smiling, for my response, and when I didn't—because I couldn't—make any, he laid his hand briefly over mine. 'I haven't embarrassed you, have I? You mustn't mind me, I'm afraid I'm not used to young girls.'

'I am not,' I said icily, 'a young girl.'

'Oh hell, I've done it again!' His rueful expression would have been comic if I hadn't felt so miserable. As it was, my only concern was to stop him thinking of me as a child, and I blurted out recklessly,

'At any rate, I'm four years older than Cathy was when she married you!'

There was a brief silence while I stared at him, aghast, watching the amusement fade from his face.

'Meaning that at least you've more sense than she had? She was courageous, though, you must give her that. Despite all the arguments about being too young to know her own mind, she was determined to go through with it. And look where it got her.'

I couldn't meet his eyes. 'Simon, I'm sorry. I didn't mean—I don't know what made me say that.'

After a moment he said shortly, 'I'm sorry, too. I shouldn't have let fly like that. It was just the old defence mechanism clicking into place. You happened to touch on rather a sore point.'

So he was still in love with her. He had been trying to be pleasant to me for her sake, and I had unaccountably rounded on him. In a last attempt to salvage the ruins of this longed-for evening, I said carefully, 'Tell me about Africa. It must have been fascinating out there.'

Gratefully he seized on the lifeline I had thrown him and the evening slid past very much on the surface, with both of us being extremely careful to avoid any subject verging on the personal. He took me home but refused my invitation to come in for a cup of coffee.

'Thank you for coming, Cherry. It couldn't have been easy for you, and I want you to know that I appreciate it. I'm sorry I was so prickly earlier on. Take care of yourself, and remember me to your parents when you write.'

As I let myself into the flat I reflected bleakly that, if David had only been on time that evening two weeks ago, I should have been spared a great deal of unhappiness—and Simon Slade what must have been a most unpleasant evening.

CHAPTER TWO

I certainly didn't expect to hear from Simon again, and when the phone rang a few days later it was a shock to hear his voice.

'I've just been given two tickets for the new play at the Apollo and wondered if you'd like to come?'

I held tightly on to the phone. It would be easy to plead a prior engagement. He would get the message and then he definitely wouldn't contact me again. I was well aware that, if I did go, I'd be in for another session of sleepless nights and allergy to the telephone.

'As a matter of fact,' he went on when I didn't speak, 'this is by way of a peace offering. I gave you rather a rough time the other evening and I've had quite a conscience about it.'

'When are they for?' I stalled.

'Sorry—Saturday evening. Are you seeing What's-his-name?'

I said slowly, 'I usually do, but we haven't fixed anything definite.'

'Then please come. We could have supper afterwards.'

Had I really ever thought I could refuse him? 'Thank you,' I said primly, 'that would be very nice.'

'Simon?' asked Sue resignedly, as I replaced

the phone.

'Yes.'

'After the last time, I'm surprised you're prepared to risk it. I've never known you so mopey.'

'He wants to apologize. Please, Sue, don't flog it.'

'Poor old David. His days are numbered, aren't they?'

I didn't reply. Miraculously, I had been given a second chance and I intended to make the most of it.

The evening was a success from the start. The play, a new comedy, was witty and amusing, Simon and I were on a completely different footing, and the quietly assessing look I'd surprised on his face was certainly not avuncular.

'You know,' he said slowly over supper, 'I didn't really expect you to come out with me at all. I never exactly endeared myself to your family, did I? No doubt I was held up as a warning—the original Big Bad Wolf.' He looked across at me. 'So why did you come, Cherry?'

I met his eyes steadily. 'Why did you ask me?' I countered.

He smiled and tapped the ash off his cigarette. 'You know, I'm not sure. Curiosity, I suppose, the first time. To see how you'd grown up, and so on. The second—well, I explained about that. I felt I'd been rather hard on you and regretted it. Those are my reasons, for what they're worth. What were yours?'

My eyes fell. 'Curiosity too,' I said after a moment.

'To find out if my teeth were big enough to gobble you up?'

I smiled. 'Something like that. I believe in living dangerously!'

He leaned back in his chair, his eyes still on my face. 'I hope you don't make a habit of that kind of remark with your other escorts. It could land you in trouble.'

'But not with you?'

'No,' he said quietly, 'you're safe enough with me. This wolf has had his teeth drawn. What about that fellow you were with?' he added suddenly. 'Is it serious?'

I shook my head, not looking at him.

'Well, take some advice from me, in my grandmother disguise. Never marry for love. Settle for affection, respect, companionship and compatibility. Believe me, you'll be much happier.' He gave a short laugh. 'End of philosophizing. Now eat your ice like a good girl. It's time I took you home.'

At the door he gave me a little bow and said formally, 'Thank you for a delightful and most enlightening evening.'

I wasn't at all sure what he meant, and lay awake most of the night trying to work it out.

16

The next time Simon phoned, it was with an invitation for an evening on which I had a long-standing date with David. I took a deep breath and crossed my fingers.

'Simon, I'd have loved to but I'm afraid I can't. I'm already going out that evening.'

'But I have the tickets. Can't you get out of it?'

I said with more dignity than truth, 'I don't want to. I'm sorry, but it would have been wiser to check with me first—before buying any tickets.'

'As you say.' His voice was clipped and, in spite of myself, I remembered Father's words about his liking his own way. 'Then perhaps you'll be kind enough to tell me when you will be free?'

'Would Tuesday do?'

'Admirably, I imagine. I'll see you then.'

Whatever the tickets had been for on Saturday, Tuesday was merely a dinner date. Simon was quiet and withdrawn, seemingly wrapped up in his own thoughts, and when he failed to respond to my light conversation, I also lapsed into silence. Eventually he roused himself sufficiently to look across at me.

'Did you enjoy yourself on Saturday?'

'Very much, thank you.'

'David again?'

So he remembered the name after all. 'Yes.'

17

'You're still seeing him, then?'

It seemed an obvious comment, but I said again, 'Yes.'

'Does he know you've been seeing me?'

'There didn't seem much point in mentioning it.'

'Afraid of making him jealous?'

'There's nothing for him to be jealous of, is there?' I asked innocently. I leaned forward. 'What is it, Simon? You're very morose this evening.'

'Yes, I'm sorry. I realize I haven't exactly been scintillating company.'

'But what's wrong?'

He straightened and met my eye. 'You couldn't be expected to remember, but today would have been our tenth wedding anniversary.'

'Oh.' I felt cold, deflated. I had begun to hope that he might have been just a little jealous of David, and all the time he had merely been missing Cathy.

'It gets very lonely sometimes. Oh hell, Cherry, I've made such a mess of everything.'

I put my hand quickly over his. 'Poor Simon.'

'And poor Cherry, being inflicted with all this when you were expecting an evening's entertainment.'

'I wish there was some way I could help, that's all.'

'Do you?' There was an odd expression in

his eyes, and my stupid heart started to hammer.

'Of course,' I stammered. 'If there's anything I can do—'

He patted my hand. 'Just put up with me when I'm in one of these self-pitying moods. Let's go, or we'll have you crying into your coffee.'

It was dark and raw outside. We turned into the narrow little side street where we had left the car, and I huddled into my coat while I waited for Simon to unlock it. He turned towards me and I took a step forward, ready to get into the car. But he said in a low voice, 'As to giving David something to be jealous about, how's this for a start?' And he pulled me into his arms. I was so surprised that I stumbled slightly. His mouth was cold and ruthlessly demanding. I clung to him dizzily, unable to believe what was happening.

After a moment he released me.

'Get inside; it's too cold to stand about.' It was too dark to see the expression on his face. Obediently I stumbled into the car. He came round and got in beside me, and lit a cigarette. Neither of us spoke. I was concentrating on trying to control the fit of trembling which shook my whole body. He started the car and we emerged from our private darkness into the full brilliance of the West End. I was waiting tensely for Simon to make some comment but he didn't. He seemed in a world of his own, occupied by his own brooding thoughts. We drew up outside the flat, and still in silence, he accompanied me to the door.

'Good night,' I whispered.

'Good night, Cherry.' He stood looking down on me, but his eyes were in shadow. He said suddenly, 'You've been very sweet. Thank you.' He bent forward and kissed my cheek. Then he turned and went quickly back to the car. My fingers were trembling so much that I had difficulty getting the key into the lock. He had driven away before I'd closed the door behind me.

* * *

The next phone call was brief and not very explicit. 'Okay for Sunday? I'll pick you up about two-thirty. Wear flat shoes.'

I turned from the telephone, met Sue's eye, and shrugged slightly. 'Two-thirty, Sunday—flat shoes.'

'Perhaps he wants you to caddy for him?' she suggested helpfully.

'Or flee with him to the coast?' pondered Lucy. ' "Once aboard the lugger—" '

'Or pick primroses in the woods?' I contributed.

As it happened, we were all wrong. When Simon called for me, and led me over to the parked car, three pairs of round, solemn eyes regarded me dubiously from the back seat. He

20

had the children with him.

Disappointment flooded over me. I didn't want to share my precious day with three children who, as I was only too well aware, had far more claim on Simon than I was ever likely to have. He was waiting, smiling slightly, for my reaction, and it wasn't quite what he'd expected.

'So you want a nanny for the afternoon! Can't you cope single-handed?' I was appalled to hear the edge on my own voice.

He started to say something, changed his mind, and remarked calmly, 'You said you hadn't seen them for some time. I thought it was a good chance to renew your acquaintance.'

But I didn't say I *wanted* to see them, I thought rebelliously. He got into the car beside me.

'Children, you remember Cherry, don't you?'

'Hello,' I said ungraciously.

'We're going to the zoo!' piped Anna, from the back seat. I closed my eyes, deciding with instant conviction that the zoo was, in the whole world, my least favourite place. I had always loathed the sight of wild creatures in cages and after all the rain of the past week the place would be like a quagmire. Flat shoes indeed; he should have specified gumboots.

'And we've got a picnic tea!' Paul

21

elaborated. Fine, fine. Dry sandwiches, no doubt, with tired lettuce and hard strips of ham curling at the edges. Unconcerned by my lack of joyous response, the children started chattering among themselves. Simon's eyes met mine in the driving mirror.

'It may never happen, you know.'

'What mayn't?'

'The disaster you're apparently expecting.'

'I was wishing,' I replied tartly, 'that I'd put on an older pair of shoes. If you'd said where we were going—'

'You wouldn't have come.'

'Would it have mattered?' I asked bitterly.

'It might have done.'

To my fury I was almost in tears. After his kiss the other evening, I had hoped for so very much from today.

'Come on, Cherry, stop sulking, there's a good girl. *Three* children are certainly as much as I can cope with.'

I tried to think of a suitable retort, but fortunately Anna leaned forward to speak to Simon and saved me the necessity. He glanced at me sideways.

'All right, I know I should have been more explicit, but I didn't want to risk your refusing to come. Now cheer up and make the best of it, for the children's sake. And mine. All right?'

'All right,' I said, slightly mollified.

'Good girl!' The battle won, Simon settled

back comfortably and turned into Regent's Park. He had got his own way again.

It wasn't until we were out of the car that I was able to take a good look at the children. James and Paul, aged nine and eight, were much of a size. Paul would probably be the taller eventually. At the moment his face was rounder and had a much younger expression than his brother's. James struck me as a very serious little boy. He rarely smiled and he kept close to Simon, his eyes never leaving his father.

Anna was small and plump and six years old, her heavy, fair hair contained in 'bunches' which swung somewhat wildly at an angle on either side of her little face. Her large grey eyes, dark-fringed, seemed too big for her small features. She clung like a limpet to Simon's hand, which left Paul and me to fend for ourselves. Accordingly, we set off in the wake of the other three. I was in an uncomfortable mood, still resentful of being put in this position and unwilling to analyze my reaction to seeing Simon surrounded by his children.

'Penguins first!' Anna was chanting.

'No, tigers!' insisted James.

'We'll see everything as it comes,' said their father, peaceably.

Before long the never-distant rain had begun again, and my new shoes developed a tightness across the instep which was crippling.

At my side, Paul kept up a steady chatter, which saved me the trouble of making conversation.

At about four, we were huddled on a bench, partly sheltered by trees, while the children dived delightedly into the picnic basket and Simon poured cups of tea for ourselves. His coat collar was turned up against the rain, his hair plastered on his forehead, but his eyes were bright with enjoyment.

'Have you a hanky, Anna?' I asked, when I could no longer overlook the need for one.

'Mummy said there's one in my raincoat pocket.' The question, as far as Anna was concerned, was academic.

'Then do you think you could use it?' I prompted. 'Can you blow your nose?'

'Of course she can blow her nose. She's not a baby.' It was James who had spoken, his eyes fixed on my face in a long, assessing look over the top of his packet of crisps.

For all her brother's confidence, Anna did not make a very good job of it, and my last shred of appetite withered away. Without thinking, I tossed my sandwich on to the grass in front of us.

'You're not supposed to feed the animals,' James said accusingly.

'There aren't any animals here.'

'The camels come past when they're giving 'rides.'

'A camel's too high off the ground to see a

24

little sandwich!' My attempt at a joke met with no response. For the first time it occurred to me that the children, or at any rate James, might resent my intrusion in the party as much as I resented theirs. None of us wanted to share Simon's attention.

'I'm still hungry,' Anna announced, when the last packet had been emptied. 'Can I have an ice cream?'

'Not if we have to queue for it,' Simon said firmly. 'Anyway, that was only a stopgap. Mrs. Charles will have supper ready when we get home.'

'Talking of going home,' I put in, 'you can drop me at the nearest tube if it's out of your way to go round by the flat.' The thought of the flat, childless, and with the gas-fire lit, was at that moment immensely appealing.

Simon looked at me in surprise. 'Didn't I explain? I was hoping you'd come back with us, and we can have a meal when the children are in bed.'

When the children are in bed. Magic words!

'You will come, won't you? You haven't made any other plans?'

'But you said you'd bath us and put us to bed!' protested Anna, obviously not pleased by the thought of my extended company.

'So I will. Perhaps Cherry will help.'

My horror must have been apparent, because James remarked, expressionlessly, 'I don't think Cherry likes children very much.'

There was an uncomfortable little silence, then Simon said briskly. 'Then it's up to you three to make her change her mind.'

'Anyway,' remarked Anna complacently, 'we're not just "children"—we're us!'

My eyes met James's. And before he could elaborate—as I knew he was going to—'I don't think she likes *us*'—I said hastily, 'I'm afraid I'm not very used to them, that's all. I never had any brothers or sisters of my own.'

'I know. Mummy told us.'

That brought me up short, and for the first time that horrible afternoon I saw the children not as Simon's but as Cathy's. 'Mummy' had told them about me. Why, and when? In general conversation, some time ago? If so, it was strange that James should have made the connection. Perhaps Simon had explained that I was 'Mummy's cousin' and that had rung a bell. But if Mummy had told them about me, they in turn would most assuredly do the same, and what would Cathy's reaction be to the news that Simon and I were seeing each other? I felt a little sick.

'Come along then,' Simon said, pushing everything back into the basket. 'Cherry's had enough and I think I have, too. Let's make our way back to the car.'

There was an instant uproar. 'But Daddy, we haven't seen the polar bears/ostriches/zebras!'

'Then we'll come back another time. The

rain's getting heavier, too. I don't want to send you all back to Yorkshire with streaming colds!'

Grumbling and protesting, the children were finally manoeuvred back to the car park and I sank thankfully into the comfortable seat, took off my scarf and shook out my damp hair.

'Your hair curls when it's wet, like Mummy's,' remarked Anna with interest.

Not wanting to become embroiled in a conversation about Mummy, I let the comment pass. The journey home was enlivened by the fact that Paul announced he felt sick, which—after what he had eaten—was hardly surprising. James confirmed that Paul often was sick in cars, and we were forced to drive home with the back window open so he could get some air. This meant that the rain blew straight in on my shoulder, which was aching naggingly by the time we reached the house.

The house where Simon and Cathy had lived for eight years was mock-Georgian in design, painted white and with enough garden on either side to keep its neighbours at a discreet distance. An imposing-looking house, in an avenue of imposing-looking houses, not too big to be difficult to run, but big enough to accommodate three children and living-in help.

As the front door was opened, a wave of

warmth lapped out over us and drew us in with a tangible welcome. Mrs. Charles, small, neat and bespectacled, hurried forward to relieve us of our dripping raincoats.

'I think the children should have their baths straight away, sir, to warm them through, and have supper in their dressing-gowns. And perhaps the young lady would like a wash too. I've put a towel for her in the second bathroom, since the children will be in the other.'

'Thanks, Mrs. Charles. This is Miss Lester, by the way, my wife's cousin. Cherry, if I ever write a book of my life, Mrs. Charles will be the one "without whom—"'

He disappeared with the children, leaving the housekeeper to show me upstairs and through the main bedroom to the bathroom that lay beyond. It was tiled in turquoise, with two mirrored walls, a low bath and a vanity unit: very obviously Cathy's choice of decor. On the vanity unit stood a bottle of after-shave and a hair brush. I looked at them for a long moment, then plunged my hands into the bowl of hot water.

By the time I had redone my make-up and brushed my hair I was feeling much more civilized. I emerged into the bedroom, taking in the fitted furniture with the gold filigree handles, the long elegant dressing-table with its bare surface. What unhappiness had this room witnessed, before Cathy and Simon finally split up?

The warm, comfortable room off the kitchen was known as the breakfast room, but at this time of day, Paul insisted on calling it the supper room. The children were seated around the table in their dressing-gowns demolishing baked potatoes sprinkled with cheese and crisp bacon. Anna's hair, brushed till it shone, hung around her shoulders like a ripple of pale silk. Simon motioned me to a chair at one end of the oval table and handed me a glass. 'It's nice to have a full table for once,' he commented. 'Usually I sit here in solitary splendour.'

No doubt I was in Cathy's place. I was tired and the warmth of the room pressed on my eyelids. I hoped the children would go to bed soon, but this, of course, they were reluctant to do, and it was eight-thirty before at last they were settled and Simon and I went to the dining-room for our own meal.

We spoke only spasmodically as we ate, both content to relax, but when the coffee had been brought in and Mrs. Charles left us alone, Simon said smilingly, 'Was the day as bad as you expected?'

'I seem to have survived.'

'Contrary to your expectations?'

I said bluntly, 'I'm not very good with children, Simon.'

'I shouldn't have dropped you among them without warning. It was sheer selfishness. I wanted you there as well.'

'You probably regretted it more than once. When are they going home?'

'Tomorrow morning.'

'The house will seem quiet. I'm sorry, Simon.'

'For what?'

'Disappointing you. I was in a foul mood; I spoilt the day.'

'No you didn't, and it was your day as much as ours.' Ours. His and the children's. 'Also, I had a particular reason for wanting you to meet each other, to see how you'd get on.'

'We didn't do too well, did we?'

'It could have been worse. Paul seemed to take to you.'

'One out of three, for trying!' I said brittlely.

He moved suddenly. 'Cherry, I haven't the remotest idea how to go about this so I might as well come straight out with it. Is there the faintest chance that you might consider marrying me?'

'*Marrying* you?' The shock reverberated in my voice.

'I know I'm not much of a bargain. There are a lot of things I'm not proud of and I haven't exactly led a monastic existence since Cathy left, but there's never been anyone I wanted to spend the rest of my life with.'

My eyes fastened on his, hoping against hope for some hint of what I longed to see there. When it failed to materialize, I said

30

flatly out of an intolerable hurt, 'Why me?'

He frowned slightly. 'I don't understand.'

'Nor do I.' My voice was shriller than I liked. 'I repeat, why me? If all you want is someone to run your house efficiently and keep you company, surely it would have been wiser to choose someone who had no connection with your first wife?'

He said uncertainly, 'I couldn't have made myself very clear. It's you I want.'

'But why?' My voice shook. 'You've been very careful to avoid any mention of love.'

'Cherry, listen.' His voice was gentle. 'I explained how I felt about that. I couldn't go through it again and there's no reason why you should either. I wouldn't wish it on my worst enemy. We get on well together, don't we? We adapt to each other's moods, and you told me there's no one else you're interested in. I know I'm rushing things rather, but I'm tired of being alone and I think we could make each other happy. I'm fond of you and I'm sure we could have a good life together. Isn't that enough?'

I couldn't speak. The silence stretched interminably between us and at last he let his breath out in a rasping sigh. 'What a bloody fool I am. Of course it isn't. God, Cherry, you must think me an idiot. How I could have imagined—' He broke off, his face white with humiliation, and I caught hold of his hand between both of mine.

'Don't look like that, Simon. It's just that—well, you might not want any more to do with love, but I do. You can't expect me to agree to such a cut and dried approach to something that should be wonderful and beautiful—' I choked to a halt and tried again. 'What I'm trying to say is that it wouldn't seem like a marriage to me, without love. Do you understand?'

'Of course I understand,' he said harshly. 'And I also understand that I haven't a hope in hell. I can't imagine what possessed me to suppose—'

'It's only the way I feel about it,' I said wildly, trying to dispel the expression in his eyes. 'I'm sure there are plenty of girls who'd be only too happy to marry you on those terms.'

His mouth twisted. 'Please don't get the impression that you were simply at the head of a list. I don't want 'plenty of girls', I want—wanted—you. But you're quite right, you're much better off without me. Why should you settle for second best? At any moment you might meet someone you could really love, if not David then someone else. It's not for me to try to talk you out of experiencing love just because I was hurt by it.' He pushed back his chair. 'After which embarrassing discussion, it only remains for me to apologize once again and take you home. I'll get your coat. It should be dry by now.'

The journey through the dark, wet night was almost unbearable. My face was frozen from not daring to relax. Occasionally Simon made stilted conversation, to which I could not reply. I knew he was as furious with me as with himself, for causing his discomfort, for allowing him, as he saw it, to make a fool of himself. For it was only his pride which was hurt. That was all my refusal had meant to him.

At last we were home. Silently he got out of the, car and came round to open the door for me.

'You won't worry about all this will you?' he said brusquely. 'Just forget it ever happened. And believe me, I'm sorry it did.'

'I'm sorry too,' I whispered, and added formally, like a child after a party, 'Thank you for asking me.' Then, because his face was so bleak and because already I was regretting having refused him, whatever the terms, I reached up, caught hold of his head between my hands and kissed him hard on the mouth. I felt him stiffen, as though all his defences were rushing into position.

'Say good-bye to the children for me,' I said—and fled.

CHAPTER THREE

A week passed, seven days divided into twenty-four hours apiece. I worked, I ate a little, sometimes I slept. One morning a somewhat affronted letter arrived from my mother: 'Cathy tells me the children saw you at the weekend. I must say I was surprised. I'd no idea Simon had been in touch with you. I strongly advise you, Cherry, to see as little of him as politeness allows.'

I wondered bleakly what report of me Cathy had received.

Then, early on Sunday evening, the doorbell rang. I stayed where I was, curled in a chair waiting for the undemanding intricacies of the television serial to occupy my mind. I heard Sue open the door, heard her say, 'I'm not at all sure she wants to see you. No, really, I don't think you should—' And then the sitting room door had opened and Simon stood there.

I didn't move. Across the room we looked at each other. He said awkwardly, 'I'm sorry to burst in like this, but I have to see you.'

When I made no reply he came across and stood looking down at me. 'Or would you rather I left straight away? It's up to you.'

'You might as well say what you came to.'

He said in a low voice, 'Then it's this. After all that patronizing rubbish I subjected you to last week, I've discovered to my cost that I do love you after all. I couldn't let you go without one last try, just in case you felt that it made a difference.'

In the tense silence the gas-fire hissed and popped gently. I didn't believe him, of course. He'd only said that because he knew my terms, but at least he was fond enough of me to risk another rebuff. For myself, I had love enough for both of us. These last miserable days had left me in no doubt of that.

He turned away abruptly. 'Well, it was a forlorn hope, but I had to give it a try.'

'Simon—'

'Well?'

I said with difficulty, 'I will marry you, if you really want me to.'

'You will? You mean it?'

'If you want me.'

'Oh. Cherry!' He pulled me up and into his arms, holding me tightly, his face in my hair. 'I know it's more than I deserve, but I'll try to make you happy.' He tipped my chin back and kissed me, slowly but thoroughly. Cathy, Mother, the children—everything faded into insignificance. I was in Simon's arms and that was the only thing that mattered.

'As a matter of fact,' I said a little later, 'I had a letter from Mother this week, warning me about you!'

His arms tightened. 'It's not going to be easy.'

'I know. There'll be scenes and recriminations and heaven knows what. It— won't hurt Cathy, will it?'

'I can't see why it should.'

'Simon, there's one thing I have to ask. Are you hoping that if you marry me you'll have more chance of getting the children back?'

He moved away from me and felt in his pocket for cigarettes. Then he said jerkily, 'I suppose I deserved that. No, Cherry, nothing I do would ever get me the children. I admit I had hoped you'd get on well with them, but I shouldn't have expected a kind of instant mother-love. They're not yours, after all.'

'But they're yours.'

'Never mind, it will be different with our own.'

'I don't want any children.' The words were as much of a surprise to me as to him. I had never put it into words before, even to myself, but I felt instinctively that the children had been the crux of the trouble between Cathy and Simon. Certainly they had been the cause of the final break, when she had refused to leave them to go to Africa with him. I couldn't afford to be tied down. I had to be with Simon always, and I daren't risk sharing the small portion of his heart that I had managed to salvage with anyone else, even our own child. Already it was divided, between Cathy, the children and me. I didn't know who had the largest share, only that I hadn't.

'Well, there's plenty of time to talk about that,' he said after a moment.

'No. Simon, we must get it straight now.' I was trembling with the enormity of the risk I had to take. 'I won't marry you under false pretences. If you want more children, you'd better choose someone else.'

He looked at me for a long moment and somehow I managed to meet his eyes. Then he smiled. 'You're a great one for ultimatums, aren't you? And you seem convinced that I have a little black book somewhere that I can just leaf through if you won't have me. I want *you* to marry me, and if those are your terms, I suppose I must just accept them, though I can't help hoping you'll change your mind. In the meantime, we'd better get down to more immediate problems. I suppose we must go and brave your parents together. So, what date shall we make it?'

'The visit home?'

'No, little goose, the wedding!'

My breath knotted in my throat. 'Shouldn't we wait till we've seen the parents?'

'I think it might be wiser to present them with a firm date. It will have to be a registry wedding, of course. So much for all your dreams of veils and orange blossom.'

'I'd realized that.' But all the orange blossom in the world hadn't helped Cathy. I had a sudden mental picture of myself handing them a silver horseshoe and hastily pushed it away. 'We'd better go up next weekend.'

'I should drop them a line first, to warn them what's in store. We don't want to cause any coronaries! So how soon will you marry me, Miss Lester?'

'The end of the month?'

'Fine.' He raised my hand to his lips and kissed the fingers.

I said tentatively, 'Will we live in the same house?'

He looked up. 'I'd assumed so. Why, have you any objections?'

'It's just that you and Cathy chose everything together and she went there as a bride.'

'You needn't worry about that; she's been well and truly exorcised by now. It's a perfectly good house, though, and apart from anything else we haven't really time to look for another place.'

'No, I suppose not. It doesn't matter.' And I gave in to Simon again without even noticing it.

He met me at work on Friday evening. I had taken my suitcase in with me and we made straight for the motorway. Apart from a brief lunch hour when we had bought the ring, it was the first time we'd been together since our engagement. I had duly written a note to my parents telling them I was going to marry Simon in three weeks' time and that we would be up to see them this weekend. I had not received a reply, but I'd hardly expected one. I was not looking forward to the next two days.

As though reading my mind, Simon said suddenly, 'You're not regretting anything, are you? There's still time to change your mind. I know I rather rushed you into it.'

'I've no regrets, but the same applies to you.'

He smiled fleetingly. 'Positively none, except that we have to face your parents!'

'You won't be too upset, will you, if they don't welcome you with open arms?'

'I'm not expecting a welcome, my love. They didn't even approve of me for Cathy, let alone their own ewe lamb. I had a tougher time with your father than I did with her mother, and that's saying something.'

'What about your own family? I seem to remember your father at the wedding, and your sister was a bridesmaid with me.'

'That's right. Caroline married an American and now lives in the States. When Father retired I was in Africa and had no idea how long I'd be there. He went out to stay with Caro and liked it so much he only came home to sell up before moving out there permanently. Mother, of course died when I was sixteen.'

'So you've no one of your own here—for moral support.'

'I've got you, haven't I?'

'Of course you have,' I said quickly.

We stopped at a service station for dinner and were on the road again within the hour. Even so, it was almost ten o'clock by the time we left the motorway for the last few miles home. And the nearer we came, the more nervous I felt. Neither of us spoke, except for Simon's occasional: 'Left here, isn't it?' Yet despite the long journey, when we finally drew up outside the house I would have welcomed another hour's drive to separate us from the imminent meeting.

The porch light was on but the curtains of the sitting room were drawn and no one peeped through, though they must have been listening for the car. We were obviously not going to be offered any help.

Simon bent quickly and kissed my cheek. 'Chin up, love, they can't eat us!'

We went up the path together. No one came to open the door. I pushed it open and called with false gaiety, 'Anybody home?'

At that the sitting room door did open and my parents came into the hall.

'Hello, Cherry.' My mother held her cheek to receive my kiss. So did Father, and after a moment he took Simon's outstretched hand. 'Well, come in, both of you. You must be tired after the long drive.'

I saw my mother's eyes flicker to the diamond on my finger, but she made no comment and I was as hurt as if it had been a child she ignored. Simon gave my hand a little squeeze as we went into the warm, familiar room.

'I've some soup on the stove,' Mother said, 'but perhaps you could do with a drink first.' She looked at Father and he went over to the cabinet and filled four glasses.

Simon said awkwardly, 'Mrs. Lester, I know this has come as a shock to you but I do hope you'll give us your blessing. I'll do everything in my power to make her happy.'

'You weren't very successful with Cathy, were you?' said my mother tightly.

'Ellen!' Father handed her the glass with a warning look. 'It's no use pretending we're glad about it,' he went on heavily, 'because of course we're not. It was a shock, to all of us. Until the children returned home we'd no idea you'd even met, let alone been carrying on a— a courtship behind our backs.'

Simon said stiffly, 'We didn't go behind anyone's back, sir. It all happened rather suddenly, that's all. I met Cherry quite by chance and it went on from there.'

'Then why didn't she mention it?' demanded Mother bitterly. 'No, I know the answer. She knew we wouldn't approve.'

'She was afraid you wouldn't, and it worried her. But in the final analysis she has her own life to lead.'

'And we're supposed to sit back and keep quiet when we see her making a terrible mistake?'

'Mother, how can you!' I burst out. 'Forget about Cathy. Just because—'

'How can I forget? I remember only too well how unhappy she was with Simon, and now you propose to go the same way!'

'If Cathy was unhappy it was at least partly her fault!' I flared. 'You never bothered to find out Simon's side of it. And don't forget it was she who left him.'

'Cherry, please!' my father interrupted heavily. 'We're not trying to antagonize you, child.'

'Then stop attacking Simon, both of you! If you're hoping to change my mind, I tell you now that it won't work!'

'But have you really had time to think about it? I can't believe that you have. The last we heard you were going around with someone called David. What happened to him?'

'Nothing. It was never serious.' I thrust out my left hand. 'Look at my ring—isn't it beautiful?' My gaze challenged them not to admire it.

'It's very lovely, yes.'

My eyes dropped from their unhappy faces. I said in a low voice, 'You will come to the wedding, won't you?'

My parents exchanged glances. Father said, 'It's late now. We can discuss all the details tomorrow. Ellen, perhaps the soup—'

'No, I must know now. Are you coming to the wedding?'

Mother wouldn't meet my eyes. 'How can I face Beth and Cathy if I do?'

'And how can you face me if you don't? Who means more to you, Cathy or I?'

Even as I spoke I knew that it was a question I should never dare to ask Simon and the knowledge was a shaft of pain. I said shakily, 'If you love me, you'll come, however you feel about it.'

Mother's mouth trembled and for a horrified moment I thought she was going to cry. But she merely said, 'We love you, Cherry. I'm sure you don't need to be told that. If you want us to be there, we'll come. Now I really must get that soup before it boils dry.'

I gave a sigh of relief and turned to Simon. He was watching me with a kind of aching tenderness. He gave me a little smile and nod of encouragement. How much more courage I should have had to withstand my parents' objections if I could have been sure of his love. But that was an area of thought I had locked away and forbidden myself to examine.

Father said tentatively, 'There's one point I think I should mention. Cathy's coming over tomorrow. She wanted to see you.'

I felt rather than saw Simon stiffen. I didn't dare to look at him. It seemed that our doom-ringed wedding had yet one more hurdle to cross.

'Did she make any comment?' I asked quietly.

'She seemed stunned, as we all were.'

'Mother said some time ago that she was going around with someone.'

'That's so, but I don't think she has any intention of marrying again.'

'That,' remarked Simon tightly, 'I can well believe.'

Mother came back with a tray and we drank the hot soup. All I wanted now was to escape to my room as soon as possible. Surreptitiously I glanced at my parents, my father with his iron-grey hair and small military moustache, to my mind the prototype of all bank managers. And Mother, with her soft hair which never looked entirely up-to-date and indeed no different from the way she had always worn it. Their unhappiness lapped the room in palpable waves and I ached to be able to reassure them, to promise that I'd be happy.

As soon as we laid down our spoons they both stood up. Mother said, 'I expect you'd just like to say good night to each other and then you can show Simon upstairs, Cherry. I've put his case in the guest room. I'll bring you both a cup of tea about eight o'clock. I hope you sleep well.'

'Good night, Mum.' I kissed her still-unresponsive cheek, and Father patted my arm as though in an attempt at apology for what he'd been unable to avoid saying. The door closed behind them.

'Phew!' Simon leaned back on the sofa.

'Give me the rack any day! Come and sit down for a minute.' He patted the cushion beside him and his arm came round me as I joined him. Wearily I leaned my head on his shoulder.

'You were wonderful, sweetheart. I didn't know you could be such a little spitfire. It made me very humble, sitting back while you fought my battles for me.'

'Two down and one to go,' I said, and felt the spasm of his hand on my shoulder.

'Yes, I feel we might have been spared Cathy's blessing.'

I looked up into his face. 'Will you mind seeing her?'

His jaw tightened. 'I haven't since the divorce. I don't imagine it will be too pleasant.'

'Not for me, either.'

'No. You're certainly having a baptism of fire, aren't you? I only hope you'll think it's been worth it!'

'You'd better guarantee that!' I said teasingly, but he didn't smile. Perhaps his thoughts were still on Cathy. I said urgently, 'Kiss me, Simon.' I held on to him, and though his arms were round me there was still that sense of reserve I was always conscious of. It wouldn't be easy to break through that, to make him learn to trust me, knowing that I shouldn't hurt him as he'd been hurt before.

'Come on, young lady, it's time you were in bed. Today has been too long by half.'

Reluctantly I stood up. 'I wish it was this

time tomorrow.'

'Me too,' he said grimly, and with Cathy once again in both our minds, we went slowly upstairs.

*　　*　　*

She came just after lunch. We'd had a lazy morning, taking our time over breakfast and going to the village for the weekend groceries. The strained atmosphere was still present, even between Simon and me. As soon as the meal was over, Father escaped to the bottom of the garden muttering about bedding plants. Mother and I washed the dishes in silence.

'Is Aunt Beth coming?' I asked, breaking it.

'No, she'll stay with the children. What did you think of them, by the way?'

'Much the same as any other children.'

'You never were one for hanging over prams, were you?' I sensed a rebuke, her words bringing back memories of Cathy's visits as a child, when she was always wanting to wheel out the neighbours' babies. Cathy had certainly been born with her full share of maternal instinct. Perhaps she had my share as well.

Simon and I were alone in the sitting room when she arrived. She came straight in and stopped abruptly just inside the door, her eyes on Simon. Then she smiled and said with remarkable composure, 'Hello, you two. I hear you're to be congratulated.'

Simon said under his breath, 'Cathy—'

I didn't seem to exist for either of them.

'The children did so enjoy their visit to the zoo,' she prattled on. 'We heard all about it, the picnic and the rain and the baked potatoes for supper. It sounded just like—'

Just like old times. That's what she'd been going to say. Simon said abruptly, 'I'm sure you'd like a word with Cherry. I think I'll join Mr. Lester in the garden.'

He brushed past her—she moved only very slightly to one side—and we were alone.

'You don't mind, do you?' I asked numbly.

'I haven't any right to mind. It was odd, though, seeing Simon just now. He looked so exactly the same, it was hard to believe that we—well, never mind that. I hope you'll be very happy together, really I do. It just never occurred to me—but then it wouldn't, would it? I suppose I never really expected him to marry again, especially when—' She broke off, colouring.

'When what?'

'Nothing. I'm sorry. I'm not thinking very straight.'

'What were you going to say?'

Her colour deepened. 'Please, Cherry, I honestly didn't mean to—'

'Cathy!'

'All right,' she said flatly, 'if you insist. I was going to say, "Especially when he wrote to me only a few months ago begging me to go back."'

I stood completely still, waiting for her words to penetrate.

She was saying quickly, 'Of course, that was when he was still in Kenya, before he met you. Still, it did make it more of a shock.'

'Did you answer his letter?' I asked expressionlessly.

'No.'

'And he didn't write again?'

'No. Look, please don't attach any importance to it. It was probably done on the spur of the moment anyway, in a fit of depression. I wish to goodness I hadn't been so stupid as to mention it.'

'Are you wishing now that you had replied?'

'No. I'd never have agreed to go back.'

'Why?'

'There were so many things we didn't see eye to eye about. We rubbed each other raw. Even so, there'll always be something between us. You can't live with someone for eight years and then shake yourself completely free of him, can you?'

'I wouldn't know. Will you ever marry again?'

'No.' She was quite definite. 'I have the children: they're all I really need.'

I heard my mother's footstep on the stairs and a moment later she joined us. The conversation became rather self-consciously impersonal and I let it flow over my head,

48

remembering Simon's clenched jaw, his soft, whispered 'Cathy!' How had he felt, seèing her again? Had he too found it hard to believe they were not still together? Wished, perhaps, that he'd written again, waited a little longer, before giving up all hope of getting her back?

After a few minutes, Cathy rose to her feet. 'I must be going. I have some shopping to do on the way home.'

'You won't stay for tea, dear?'

'No, I—think it would be better if I didn't. Say goodbye to Uncle and Simon for me.' She opened her handbag and drew out a parcel wrapped in tissue paper. 'I'll be thinking of you on the thirtieth, Cherry. Here's a little wedding present, with my best wishes.'

It was an ivory figurine, beautifully carved. I thought how well it would look in the Surrey sitting room, and realized the same idea must have occurred to Cathy. She kissed me good-bye, her face cool and smooth against my flushed one.

'Tell Simon he—you can have the children any weekend if you give me enough notice. I had promised they'd spend part of the Easter holidays with him, but I suppose you'll hardly be back from your honeymoon. Perhaps we'd better leave it till half-term. You can let me know nearer the time.'

To avoid any probing queries from my mother, I walked with her to the gate and then round the side of the house to where Father was on his knees digging in the new plants while Simon leaned against the wall watching him in silence. Poor Simon: this had been the only place to flee to and, judging by my father's unresponsive back, it hadn't been much of a sanctuary.

'She's gone,' I said briefly, and saw him relax a little. Father rose stiffly to his feet, dusting down his trousers.

'All this female chatter has made your mother overlook my cup of tea. I'll go and remind her.'

He walked away from us, down the garden. I moved a clod of earth off the path with the toe of my shoe.

'Well?'

'Well what?'

'What did she say? Did she give you ten good reasons for not marrying me?'

'No, she hoped we'd be very happy.'

'Hoped, but doubted.' He looked at me closely. 'She said something to upset you. What was it?'

'Nothing.'

He gave an exclamation of impatience. 'Look, if we're not going to be completely honest with each other we won't even get to first base.'

'In that case, why didn't you tell me you'd written to her recently asking her to come back?'

There was a ringing in my ears. My nostrils

registered the smell of wet earth and the sharp smoky scent of spring bonfires. Above the ringing and the shouts of children in a nearby garden, my ears strained to catch his smallest reaction.

He said quietly, 'We haven't discussed anything that transpired between Cathy and me, so why should I have singled that out? It all happened before we met, anyway.'

'But the fact remains that as recently as a few months ago you wanted her back.' My voice rang with accusation. 'I was very much a second best, wasn't I?'

His face softened. 'Is that what's worrying, you? It needn't, love, it's not that at all. The fact was I was alone and depressed out there. and at such times you tend only to remember the good times. I wrote in the heat of the moment and regretted doing so as soon as I'd posted it. Fortunately she didn't reply. It would never have worked, we'd just have opened old wounds. Much better to make a clean break.'

'It's hardly a clean break when you're marrying her cousin.'

'I'm not marrying "her cousin", I'm marrying you.' He tipped his head back and blew a cloud of smoke towards the spring sky. 'How soon can we leave? I've had enough of the reproachful looks and pregnant silences, and there are plenty of things awaiting our attention at home—the details of the wedding among them. I imagine you'd like your flatmates to be there? The only people I'll invite myself are the Edwardses. You probably won't remember them, but Tom was my best man and they've been very good to me over the last couple of years. Counting your parents, that will make eight of us altogether. I thought we'd have lunch somewhere and then, having done our duty by them, we'll be free to escape.'

'And where will we escape to?'

'Would Paris be all right? I'm afraid I can only manage a week at this short notice but we should be able to get away for a holiday later in the year.'

'That sounds lovely.' I tried to inject some enthusiasm into my voice, but the recent hurt was still only just below the surface and I felt him glance at me.

'Always assuming,' he added drily, 'that you still want to marry me. Or has Cathy changed your mind after all?'

He spoke lightly but, in my turn, I detected the underlying insecurity and reached quickly for his hand. 'No, of course not. It'll be all right, won't it, Simon? It will work?'

His hand tightened on mine. 'Oh, it'll work all right,' he said grimly. 'I've no intention of failing a second time.'

CHAPTER FOUR

The weekend up north had left me with a bruised feeling. Despite his reassurance, I felt that everyone was expecting Simon's second marriage to go the same way as his first and that it would only be a matter of time. I even suspected that Lucy and Sue were of the same opinion, though they did their best to hide it from me. When we called on Helen Edwards, however, she had no such scruples.

Tom and Helen were considerably older than I was. They had two sons at boarding school and lived in what Tom alluded to as 'a most amusing mews' off Kensington High Street. It was a delightful setting, an oblong, cobbled courtyard in the centre and freshly-painted houses on three sides, each with its white balcony and a brass lantern outside the front door.

As she took my hand I found Helen's shrewd scrutiny somewhat discomfiting, but there was worse to follow.

'Come upstairs and take your coat off,' she instructed, firmly leading me away from where Tom was greeting Simon. 'Now—' she sat down on the bed as I moved uncertainly towards the dressing-table. 'Tell me why you imagine you can make Simon happy when Cathy failed.'

My startled eyes went to her face and she smiled slightly. 'I've shocked you, haven't I? I meant to. Look, my dear, I've no right to talk to you like this except that I happen to be very fond of Simon. You might not realize it, but the failure of his first marriage left very deep marks. He couldn't take it a second time.'

My heart was thundering under the unexpected onslaught, but I tried to steady my voice. 'You seem very sure it won't work.'

She moved impatiently. 'Let's be realistic about it. You're far too young for him, to start with. How can you expect to cope with all those dark moods he's subject to? Believe me, six months of marriage and you'll be running home to mother. Much better to back down now while there's still time.'

'You don't seem to have a very high opinion of me—or of Simon, for that matter, for all you say you're so fond of him.'

She studied me in the mirror as I made distracted gestures towards tidying my hair. 'You look rather like Cathy, don't you? Family resemblance, I suppose.'

'Meaning that's probably why he chose me?'

Her face softened as, despite myself, I heard my voice quiver. 'My dear, I'm being brutal, I know I am, but I'm just trying to get behind the glamour and make you face up to the truth. Because Simon *is* a glamorous figure, I quite realize that. Handsome, enigmatic, unhappy. But underneath he's desperately unsure of himself. He needs someone strong, to help him build up his self-esteem again. He went through a stage of drinking very heavily, you know, when Cathy left him. We were seeing a lot of him at that time, so believe me I know what I'm talking about. You'd be much better off with some nice uncomplicated boy your own age.'

I turned to face her, my fingernails digging into the palms of my hands. 'Helen, I don't really see why I should have to justify myself to you, but you might be surprised to learn that this isn't just a casual let's-give-it-a-try marriage for me. I've loved Simon since I was twelve years old and there's never been anyone else. I'm stronger-willed than I look, perhaps, but I tell you now that I have no intention of letting you or anyone else take him away from me. I'll fight for him if I have to. So can we please go downstairs now, before I say more than I should.'

For a moment her eyes held my defiant gaze. 'Well, good for you!' she said slowly. 'Perhaps Simon knows what he's doing after all.' She stood up. 'I've given you a nasty few minutes, but at least we both know where we stand now. If you're that determined to make a go of it, I'm right behind you. The best of luck!'

She held out her hand and after a second's hesitation I took it. Then, glad to escape, I followed her back down the stairs. A truce had been called but I knew I still had to prove myself.

The rest of the evening passed without incident. The dinner table was festive with flowers and candles, the meal itself a small masterpiece. The old French cookery book would have to be pored over before I should dare to invite them in return, and I doubted if I should ever attain Helen's easy graciousness, her attention to every detail. I wish I could like her, I thought forlornly. Even more, I wished that she liked me.

Her husband Tom, though, was a different case altogether. He was placid and kindly and, to my mind, intensely dull, but it was obvious that he thought well of everyone and that despite his wife's reservations it would never occur to him that our marriage should be other than happy. I was very grateful to Tom that evening.

When it was time for us to go, Helen laid her cheek against mine and kissed the air. 'I'm so glad we had our little talk, dear. You won't forget what I said, will you?'

She turned to kiss Simon while I submitted to Tom's bumbling, well-meant caress. Then we were out on the cobblestones, turning the large car in the small space and driving through the archway while they stood framed in the lighted doorway, waving.

But suppose she was right after all? I thought, in sudden panic. During her attack I had instinctively risen to defend myself. But now, alone with Simon in the dark, I had a moment of ice cold doubt. Would I really be capable of holding him, when even now I was unsure of his love for me? Would I always be able to deflect the doubts and worries which were bound to assail him from time to time? Suppose Helen was right, and the best thing I could do for Simon was to withdraw now, before the final step was taken?

I felt him glance at me. 'You're very quiet, Cherry.'

I said in a rush, 'I was just wondering if you were doing the right thing in marrying me.'

My eyes were tightly shut but I felt the car swerve fractionally. Then he drew in to the side of the road and switched off the engine. I opened my eyes nervously. 'What are you doing?'

He said very quietly, 'It seems this is something that needs to be talked out carefully, and I can't give it my full attention when I'm driving. Now, am I right in guessing that what you really mean is that you wonder if *you're* doing the right thing?'

I shook my head wordlessly.

'Cherry love, if you have any doubts—'

'I haven't,' I said quickly, 'but Helen certainly has.'

He frowned. 'Helen? What the hell has she got to do with it?'

'She gives our marriage six months at the

outside.'

There was a pause; then Simon said levelly, 'How pleasant to have the confidence of one's friends! Are you telling me she was trying to warn you off?'

'Only for your sake. She didn't seem to think I'm—mature enough for you.'

He reached for my hand. 'And you began to wonder if she was right?'

I said in a low voice, 'I couldn't bear you to be hurt again.'

'Oh Cherry!' Regardless of the passing traffic he pulled me roughly against him. 'Look, honey, I have good reason to be grateful to Tom and Helen. I turned to them when I had nowhere else to go, and they helped me through a very bad time. All the same, that doesn't give them the right to check-out the girl I want to marry, and Helen had no business upsetting you like this. Because it's you I want, you know. I'd hoped I'd finally managed to convince you of that.'

Because, as Helen had hinted, I had a look of Cathy?

Outside the flat his good night kiss, though tender, stopped, as always, fractionally short of committing himself. My parents—Cathy—Helen—all of them full of doubts and all of them, perhaps, knowing Simon better than I did. Closing my mind to such disloyalties I hurried into the flat.

The following evening, Simon called for me and we loaded the car with my books and records, and such clothes as I shouldn't be needing again until after the wedding. Then we drove over to Surrey to disgorge them in their new surroundings. But as I methodically began to hang up the dresses in the wardrobe allotted to me—Cathy's, of course—memories of her were everywhere: in the pleated lampshades, the deep-piled scatter rugs, the painting over the fireplace. Surrounded as I was by all these instances of her, how could I hope to exorcise her?

'Anything wrong, love?' Simon had come in behind me and slipped an arm round my shoulders.

'I'm not sure that I like having to fit into the space Cathy left.' But wasn't that, after all, exactly what I was proposing to do?

'Cherry love, this is something that has to be faced. The past is finished with. It can't hurt us any more, but all the same it's rather pointless to try to deny that it ever happened.'

I sighed. 'Yes, you're right, of course. I'm just being silly.'

I hadn't heard any more from my family beyond a brief note confirming that they had booked a hotel room for the nights of the twenty-ninth and thirtieth, and would be at the registry office at eleven-thirty. There was nothing else they could say, after all. It had already been said. Simon had sent a cable to his father and sister, and they phoned at once, very pleased with the news. I wished that Caroline were nearer, remembering the dark, pretty fifteen-year-old who had stood beside me at that other wedding. Surely she would have been an ally, and I felt badly in need of one.

The last two weeks passed in a rush of shopping for my trousseau, ordering flowers, having a farewell lunch with the girls at the office, and a hundred other things. Throughout, Lucy and Sue were there when needed, ready to soothe or advise. Several times I surprised them regarding me with a mixture of apprehension and pity. They knew as well as I did that I was much more in love with Simon than he with me, and in their opinion that was the wrong way round.

'Now,' I said, the night before the wedding when my dress, swathed in tissue paper, was hanging on the cupboard door, 'your main job tomorrow is to protect me from Helen Edwards! I shall be in a highly emotional state and quite incapable of standing up for myself.'

'I forgot to tell you, Cherry,' Lucy broke in, 'I bumped into David at lunch time.'

For a moment I actually had to think who David was.

'He was quite put out about the wedding! Said darkly that he'd always thought there was more in it than met the eye!' Lucy's voice took on the sullen note I had heard so often in David's.

'Poor boy, I'd forgotten all about him. Still, his heart isn't broken, that's for sure, though I appreciate it will be inconvenient for him to have to start educating someone else to the intricacies of foreign films!'

'You will keep in touch with us, won't you?' Lucy said wistfully.

'Of course I shall. You must come over and have dinner when we get back from Paris—a dress rehearsal for the meal I'll serve to the Edwardses!'

'Soft of official tasters,' Sue suggested. 'But don't let this woman get on top of you. After all, you've got Simon. Surely that's all that matters.'

If I really had him, it was all that would ever matter.

* * *

It was a completely unreal day. I woke early to hear rain on the windows and was unable to believe that this was the last time I should wake in this room—the last time I should wake anywhere as Cherry Lester.

The early rain blustered away, giving place to a sky of racing white clouds and an occasional threatening black one. This was my special day and I intended to savour each separate minute of it, to be relived at leisure.

The car arrived and the three of us drove through the streets of London to the grey building I had seen on so many newsreels behind newly-married celebrities. This time it was Simon who was waiting there, with my parents and Tom and Helen.

The ceremony itself seemed shockingly brief to ears long attuned to the traditional church service. I wondered for a panic-stricken moment if I were really married, staring down at my hand as Simon slipped on the ring. Only seconds later, it seemed, he and I were shaking confetti off our hair in the first of the three cars en route for the hotel. There was cold ham and wedding cake and champagne, and Mother wiping her eyes and Helen watching me.

Then another car, this time rushing us to the airport. I sat with hands clenched tightly in my lap, watching the heavy planes circling overhead. Soon we'd be up there with them, my husband and I. I turned wonderingly to Simon and found he was watching me.

'You look very beautiful, Mrs. Slade,' he said softly.

'Simon—I can't believe—'

'I know, sweetheart, I know.'

I wondered how many other honeymoon couples the driver had taken out to the airport. He kept his eyes discreetly on the road. Had the other brides felt as unsure of themselves as

I did, or had they been full of happy confidence? I reached out a hand to Simon and he took it tightly in his.

Heathrow airport, confusing at the best of times, was an extension of this dream which was half nightmare: voices booming through loudspeakers, jostling crowds, and as many languages as the Tower of Babel. Then we were at Charles de Gaulle airport and there was the drive into Paris, the sumptuous dinner amid the gay Parisians, and finally, most unreal of all, the flower-filled bedroom, and Simon and I alone at last.

I lay awake for a long, long time, while the sounds of Paris drifted up to me, and all the kaleidoscopic pieces of this terrifying, wonderful day spun crazily round inside my head. My heart ached with love for the man who lay sleeping beside me. Please let me make him happy. Help me, please.

As though aware of the force of my concentration, he stirred in his sleep, threw an arm across my body, and murmured clearly, 'Cathy!'

*   *   *

Our honeymoon in Paris was no doubt like everyone else's. We strolled arm-in-arm under the bridges, ate at little Provençal restaurants and danced cheek-to-cheek at the *Moulin Rouge*. Simon was as tender and considerate as any other bridegroom—and more handsome than most, I thought proudly. The chestnuts were in bloom along the Champs Elysées, the Bois de Boulogne was lacy with young, green leaves, and April in Paris was all that it was supposed to be. Resolutely I locked away all thoughts of Cathy and the children. Time enough to brace myself when we returned home.

And, of course, all too soon we were home. Mrs. Charles welcomed us with flowers and a hot meal, and the comfortable house was a pleasant place to relax in after the tiring journey . . . even if it still didn't feel like home.

'Are you going to keep Mrs. Charles?' I asked Simon over dinner. 'If she does all the work, what shall I do all day?'

'It's really up to you, dear. She can do as much or as little as you like. See how it goes for a while. Her son lives in the village and helps in the garden sometimes, though don't let that stop you if you ever feel like weeding! Once Easter's over we'll invite some of the neighbours round.'

I said hesitantly, 'I suppose they all knew Cathy?'

'Of course.'

'I'm sure they had a lot more in common with her than they'll have with me—children and so on.'

'Cherry—' He hesitated, not looking at me. 'You didn't really mean it, did you, what you said about not having children?'

'Yes,' I answered quietly, 'I'm afraid I did.'

'Can you tell me why?'

'I just don't want them, that's all.' I couldn't admit my own precariousness. 'I've never particularly cared for them.'

'But your own—'

'No. Simon. You promised. Look, you have children, so I'm not really depriving you. They can come to stay as often as you like.'

He was watching me with a puzzled frown. 'Is it the actual birth that worries you? Because you know these days—'

'No, it isn't that. I know it seems unnatural to you, especially after Cathy, but I can't help it. I just don't want them.' Nothing that could ever come between us, nothing that could dissipate the small share of his love that was mine alone.

He said with a little sigh, 'Well, it's early days yet. You might change your mind.'

I didn't reply.

The following day, Simon went back to work and the day stretched emptily ahead of me. I was glancing at the paper after breakfast—an unheard of luxury at that time in the morning—when Mrs. Charles came to inquire what I should like for lunch and dinner.

'Oh, don't worry,' I told her. 'I'll go and do the shopping later.'

She hesitated. 'Just as you wish, of course,

65

madam, but Mrs. Slade always left the day to day shopping to me.'

Had she but known it, that crystallized my decision. I said pleasantly, 'Then we'll have a change of routine, shall we? I must find my way around, anyway. Where are the nearest shops?'

She gave me the required directions and then left me. But after a moment, my concentration broken, I dropped the paper to the floor. The small breakfast room was warm with morning sunshine and through the door leading to the kitchen I could hear Mrs. Charles filling the sink to wash the breakfast things. Lucy and Sue would already have left for work and be strap-hanging en route to the city. I wondered a little forlornly whether they had had any replies to their advertisement for someone to take my place.

I stood up purposefully, casting around for something to occupy me, and remembered with relief that we had not unpacked properly the previous evening. I went upstairs, trailing my hand along the bannister.

Simon's pyjamas were thrown on his chair, the bed was just as we had flung out of it. I made it slowly and carefully, plumping up the pillows and smoothing the counterpane. Simon's case lay on the floor, open, some of the contents scattered beside it. I knelt down and started to fold shirts and sweaters. When everything was tidily away and the case empty

I ran my hand round the inside pockets for a final check and my fingers encountered a piece of stiff paper. I drew it out and found myself looking down at a snap of Cathy and the children. So they had been with us on our honeymoon after all. Or had the snap been pushed there long ago and simply forgotten? It wasn't something I could ask.

I sat back on my heels and looked at it more closely. Cathy was, in fact, scarcely visible, since she was holding Anna and the child's arm was obscuring her face. Judging by the ages of the children, it must be three or four years old. Carefully I replaced it in the pocket and snapped the case shut.

It was still only just after nine. I had never known time to pass so slowly. I wandered across the landing and pushed open the door of Anna's room. It looked as though she had only just left it, the small bed neatly made, an old book on the table beside it. But the cupboard and drawers were, of course, empty.

The boys' room had the same expectant air. On a table was a model car which I remembered Paul playing with the day at the zoo. Probably it had rolled under the bed and been found later by Mrs. Charles when she was dusting. I picked it up. The paint was chipped and one tyre missing. Somehow it filled me with a sense of melancholy. I put it back on the table and went out again. Perhaps some time, when things were less strained, I could invite

Mother and Father to stay with us.

I went downstairs to the kitchen, holding back an absurd impulse to knock. Mrs. Charles was peeling potatoes. I said tentatively, 'Perhaps you could give me an idea of what we're running short of?'

'Yes, madam, I have a list here.' She wiped her hands on her apron and reached behind the clock for a piece of paper. 'I've tried to keep the things needed from each shop together. I hope you can read it.'

I was putting on my coat when the doorbell rang. A red-haired young woman stood on the step smiling at me.

'You must be Mrs. Slade. I'm Sally Denver from next door but one. I saw your husband drive off this morning and wondered if perhaps you'd like a lift to the shops?'

'That is kind of you.' I picked up my bag and pulled the door shut behind me. The early morning coolness was giving way to warmth as we went down the path.

'I always think the first few weeks in a new area are difficult, until you get to know people. We're having a few friends round for drinks on Saturday evening and were wondering if you and Simon would like to come?'

'I'm sure we'd love to. Thank you very much.'

She opened the car door for me. 'If there's any rubbish on the floor, just kick it out of the way. It's usually knee-deep in sweet papers!'

I smiled. 'I gather you have children.'

'Twin girls of eight. A real handful, I can tell you, and both of them ginger like me! My poor husband was appalled! "What have I done to deserve ginger twins?" he said. But he adores them, of course.'

Of course. My smile became a little strained. Sally Denver flicked a glance towards me.

'They're the same age as Paul, so they used to play with the boys occasionally. I suppose you know the children?'

I said steadily, 'Oh yes. As a matter of fact, Cathy is my cousin.'

'Really?' Her surprise was transparent. She went on quickly, 'I'm sorry—I didn't realize—I mean—' She broke off and her face flamed. 'Now you'll think I was only wanting to pump you,' she said miserably. 'It wasn't like that at all.'

'I know it wasn't, but as you can imagine it does make things a bit more complicated. From my parents' point of view, for one thing.'

'Yes, I can see that. How awful for you.'

'I met Simon quite by chance.' It was important to establish that fact. 'We just ran into each other in London, soon after he came home, and—it went on from there. At first I think he just wanted news of Cathy and the children.'

'How is Cathy?'

'Quite composed. A lot more than we were.

She's very—self-sufficient.'

'Yes,' Sally said reflectively. 'She always gave me that impression. She never wanted any help with the children. The rest of us would meet each other's kids from school if one of us was going to be late back from town—that kind of thing. But not Cathy. It was a point of honour with her always to be there, never to depend on anyone else seeing to the children. Even Simon,' she added after a moment.

We'd driven into a busy street now, flanked with shops, and she parked the car.

'You'll find it's quite a good little shopping pitch. The butcher at the bottom of the hill is marginally cheaper than the one over there, otherwise prices are much the same everywhere. Is there anything else I can help with?'

'I don't think so, thanks. I'll enjoy wandering around and finding out where everything is.'

'If you like we could meet in about an hour for a coffee? There's a little room behind the cake shop.'

'Thanks—that'd be lovely.'

'Then I'll run you back home. By the way. I really can't go on calling you "Mrs. Slade"!'

'Sorry—it's Cherry.'

She glanced at her watch. 'Okay, Cherry— see you in the café about ten-thirty.'

I set off with my shopping basket, light of

heart. Sally's offer of friendship was very welcome. Perhaps my new neighbours wouldn't after all resent me on Cathy's behalf, but I should have to accept that they'd be curious.

It was just ten-thirty when I went through the cake shop to the café beyond. A buzz of conversation met me from the dozen or so little tables crowded together. Sally called, 'Cherry—over here!' and I threaded my way over to join her. She was sitting with a dark-haired girl who had a small child on her knee.

'Cherry, this is Sylvia Parkes, from Number 23.'

I sat down and we exchanged inconsequential chatter for a few minutes until Sylvia left us.

'Her husband's the local G.P.,' Sally informed me. 'He has a group practice just across the road from here.' She finished her coffee. 'Well, if you're ready I'd better be getting back. Have you got your Hot Cross Buns? Good Friday tomorrow!'

'Don't forget Saturday,' she reminded me when she dropped me at the gate. 'About seven-thirty.'

I told Simon about the invitation as soon as he came home. To my surprise he wasn't as pleased as I'd expected. 'It'll be a bit of an ordeal, I'm afraid. I suppose they all want a look at you.'

'But you were thinking of having people

here. What's the difference?'

'I'd only have invited one or two couples at a time, so as not to overwhelm you. I know the Denvers' parties; the world and his wife will be there.'

'She said "a few friends."'

Simon laughed. 'We can but hope. Anyway, if you can stand it, I can. I'm glad you met Sally, she's a nice girl. What else have you been doing today? Did you miss me?'

'Yes, I missed you,' I said simply. The house was empty without him.

'Never mind, we've four days together before I have to go back to work and I intend to enjoy every minute of it. For a start, what's for dinner?'

As we went through to the dining room I was full of happy confidence. We had a long weekend in front of us, I had made a new friend, and there was a party to look forward to. Perhaps my misgivings about being Mrs. Simon Slade were not well-founded after all.

CHAPTER FIVE

The Denvers' house on Easter Saturday was, as Simon had predicted, bursting at the seams. Sally welcomed us at the door and passed us over to her husband Bill, who handed us each a glass and waved an arm towards an open door from which rose a hum of voices.

'Go on in, Simon. You'll know most people—perhaps you could introduce Cherry? I'm rather bogged down at the moment, being barman.'

'Of course.' Simon took my arm and steered me into the crowded room. Several people came forward to greet us and soon I was completely bewildered by all the names and faces that were presented to me. Sylvia, the girl from the café, was there and her husband Jeremy, the doctor. I liked him at once—a dark, quiet man with thoughtful grey eyes. I wondered if he had brought Cathy's children into the world.

A very tall man in glasses was bearing down on us. 'Simon! Long time no see! How's everything?'

'Fine, thanks. Dennis, may I introduce my wife—'

'Ah yes, Cathy, isn't it? I've heard a lot about you!'

'Cherry,' I corrected quietly, hanging on to my smile. Simon seemed incapable of speech. Dennis whoever-he-was said, 'Oh, my mistake. Delighted to meet you, anyway. We must fix a game of golf, one of these days, Simon!' And he moved away, blissfully unaware of the minor explosion he had triggered off.

Simon said in a strained voice, 'Sweetheart, I'm sorry. I hardly ever see him—he couldn't have known—'

'It's all right,' I said brightly. 'It was bound to happen sooner or later.'

In fact it happened again, a few minutes later. A man we had been speaking to introduced us to another couple: 'Have you met Simon and Cathy Slade? They live just up the road.'

My smile became more fixed and I was uncomfortably aware of Simon's quietness. I also noticed, unwillingly, that his glass was never allowed to become more than half empty before it was topped up again. It was impossible to estimate how much he was drinking, but I was pretty sure it was too much. The hot, smoky atmosphere made my eyes smart and I began to wonder how soon we could slip away. Someone from across the room called to Simon, and as I tried to move with him we were separated. For a moment I felt a ridiculous sense of panic. Then a quiet voice said at my side:

'Cherry, isn't it? You look in need of rescue! Can I get you a drink?'

I drew a long breath and looked up into the quietly concerned face of Jeremy Parkes. I said a little unsteadily, 'It's not a drink I need so much as a breath of fresh air.'

'Let's see if we can find it, then.' He took my arm and steered me towards the door, the crowds miraculously parting before him, like the waters of the Red Sea.

'We'll go and sit in the kitchen for a while.'

he said calmly. 'Sally won't mind. She knows I can only take so much of her infernal parties.'

The hammering of my heart was abating.

'Sit down and I'll get you a glass of lemonade. Now, is that better?'

'Much, thank you.'

'I was afraid you were going to pass out in there. One needs to get acclimatised to these dos. Sally's motives are always of the best, bless her, but she is inclined to drop one in at the deep end—quite unintentionally, of course.'

He inspected my face with almost professional interest. 'Are you settling down all right, or is it too soon to ask?'

'I'm all right. I don't know about Simon.'

He frowned. 'How do you mean?'

'I don't think it was very easy for him to hear me called 'Cathy' twice this evening, and I'm rather afraid he's drinking too much.'

I hadn't intended to say that, but Jeremy Parkes didn't look surprised. 'No more than anyone else, I imagine. I should think it's worse for you than it is for him.'

'Not if he still loves her,' I said, without stopping to think, and then looked up fearfully, wondering what this stranger must think of me.

He said gently, 'You mustn't torture yourself like this, you know. Of course he doesn't still love her, or he would hardly have married you.'

'Perhaps I was the nearest he could get to her,' I said, and was immediately appalled by the logic of my words.

'The nearest—? I don't understand.'

'I'm her cousin.'

'Ah! Poor Cherry, torn in half by conflicting loyalties. Forget Cathy, concentrate on Simon and ignore all these fools who call you by the wrong name. It couldn't matter less.'

I said, 'You're not a psychiatrist, by any chance?'

He laughed. 'Nothing so grand, I assure you.'

'You've helped me, anyway. Thank you.'

'A pleasure,' he said gravely. 'As to Simon's drinking, don't attach too much importance to it. At least he doesn't have to drive you home! He went through rather a bad patch, I know, but he's over it now. Come on, we'll see if we can rout him out.'

We emerged into the hall just as Simon came out of the other room. 'Ah, I was wondering where you were. Been taking her pulse, Jeremy?'

'No, we just escaped for some air and a glass of lemonade. Cherry was finding the going a bit hard.'

'I've had enough, too. Are you ready to go, Cherry?'

'If you are.'

Jeremy said, 'I'll go and see if I can find Sylvia. The baby sitter has to be home by eleven. I'm so glad to have met you, Cherry.' His eyes conveyed a warm message of encouragement.

We found Bill and Sally and said our good-byes. To my relief, Simon gave no sign of having had too much to drink. Of course, I'd no idea how much he was used to. Once again it came back to how little I really knew about him.

We walked in silence the hundred yards or so down the road and turned into our own gateway. Simon locked up and I went straight upstairs. I heard him go into the sitting room and wondered anxiously if he was pouring himself yet another drink.

I was in bed by the time he came up, propped against the pillows with a book in my hand, but my mind still full of the evening at the Denvers'.

'Well, what did you think of the neighbours?'

'There were rather too many to sort out, as you'd said, but they seemed very pleasant.'

'Except for that fool Dennis Calby. And Peter, too. He should have known better—it was just a slip of the tongue.' He pulted off his tie and went through to the bathroom, but the incidents evidently stayed to his mind because when he returned and started to undress he continued the conversation as though there had been no break in it.

'You'd really think people would be more

careful. They ought to know the position is tricky enough already without additional thoughtlessness. You weren't too upset, were you?'

'Were you?' I countered.

He turned to look at me. His face was tightly drawn and his eyes burning. I said softly, 'Oh, Simon!' and held out my arms. He moved swiftly towards me, his hands gripping my bare shoulders, his head on my chest. I said ridiculously, 'It's all right, darling, it's all right.'

I could feel his ragged, uneven breathing through my thin nightdress. Gently I ran my fingers over his hair and soothingly massaged the taut muscles at the back of his neck. I felt him begin to relax, his breathing grew deeper and more even and, slightly to my surprise, I realized he was asleep. Disturbing him as little as possible I pulled the quilt over him and, still with my arm around him, reached up to switch off the light.

The next few weeks passed pleasantly and uneventfully. I went shopping most mornings, enjoying the walk if Sally didn't happen to overtake me in the car, and usually looking in at the café before starting home. Although my memories of the introductions at Sally's party remained blurred, I found that a number of people remembered meeting me there, and gradually I was able to sort them out and recognize them when I met them outside. Simon didn't refer to the party again but the memory of his falling asleep in my arms was one that I treasured, since it seemed to show that I was, after all, able to comfort him.

Then Cathy's letter arrived. I recognized the writing on the envelope before Mrs. Charles had even put it on the table and was aware of an instinctive bracing.

Simon opened it and said with studied nonchalance, 'Cathy's reminding us of the arrangement to have the children here at half-term. You won't mind, will you?'

'Of course not. How long will they stay?'

'Just the week, I imagine.' A week, when one afternoon had proved too long!

'It'll fall largely on you to entertain them, love,' he went on a little diffidently. 'I'll have the spring bank holiday at home, but I'll have to be at work the rest of the time.'

'I'll enjoy having them to myself,' I lied brightly. 'It will give me a chance to get to know them.'

They arrived on the Saturday evening and Simon and I went into London to meet them. As before, they had travelled down with a friend of Cathy's who was visiting relations in Kent. It was arranged that we should deliver them back into her keeping the following Saturday afternoon. Anna and Paul were wild with excitement and even James's eyes were bright, though he didn't say much.

'I think it might be as well if Paul sat in the front, Cherry,' Simon remarked as we came out of the station. 'We don't want a repetition of the journey home from the zoo!'

'All right,' I said meekly, taking my place in the back with Anna and James. The insidious displacement had already begun.

'Will there be baked potatoes for tea?' Anna asked, bouncing up and down until I felt I should shortly be obliged to dispossess Paul of the front seat. . . for the same reason.

'I don't think so, tonight,' I said, my hand on her knee momentarily holding her still. 'But you can have them another evening, if you like.'

'*Every* other evening!' Anna declared positively.

'No,' Paul protested, squirming round to glare at his sister. 'Sometimes we want sausages and Mrs. Charles's chips.'

'What's so special about Mrs. Charles's chips?' I inquired laughingly.

'She makes the children fritters in batter,' Simon explained. 'They're always known as Mrs. Charles's chips. '

Family lore, I thought bleakly. Given time, I should learn it all. It wasn't being deliberately withheld.

'Can I go riding, Daddy?' Anna demanded. 'Mummy said you might take me to Mr. Dobby's. Will they still have Patch, do you think?'

'You can't remember Patch!' Simon said emphatically. 'You were only four. Did

Mummy tell you about him?'

'Of *course* I remember him!' Anna protested indignantly. 'I've got a photograph of him on my dressing table!'

'Silly old horses!' said Paul with loftly masculine disdain.

'They're *not* silly, they—'

'Do you ride, Cherry?' Simon asked over his shoulder.

'Not very well.'

'Could you stand taking Anna to the stables a couple of times?'

'Every day!' said Anna decidedly. It appeared that she had the makings of an all-or-nothing girl.

'Not every day,' said Simon firmly, 'but when Cherry is kind enough to take you. What do you boys want to do?'

'Go to the woods,' said James promptly, 'and feed the squirrels.'

'Go to a football match,' Paul suggested.

'Silly, it's cricket now. You don't want to watch *cricket*!'

'Yes, I do,' said Paul stubbornly.

Simon remarked peaceably, 'When we get home you can all make a list of what you'd like to do—within reason; that is!—and we'll do our best to fit in as much as possible.'

Mrs. Charles greeted them like long-lost fledglings. During the next couple of days I was to note that they tended to ask her permission rather than mine as to what they could have to eat, or even when they need go to bed. To be fair, she usually referred them back to me, though I was aware that the situation did not displease her.

'You must ask Mrs. Slade that, lovie,' I heard her tell Anna on one occasion. Anna surveyed me with interest.

'Mummy's Mrs. Slade. Are you Mrs. Slade too? I didn't know there was more than one.'

'Just think of me as Cherry,' I said quickly.

Simon was home for their first two days and he devoted all his time to amusing them. It was a brllliantly hot weekend and deck chairs and hammocks were brought out from winter storage. In the dusty rafters of the garage Paul found a punctured paddling pool and this also had to be dragged out, repaired, cleaned, inflated and filled. For the rest of that week it stood soggily in a corner of the garden gently oozing so that the surrounding grass quickly became saturated.

'I'll take them out for the afternoon,' Simon said on Sunday. 'You have a rest while you can.'

I knew this was outwardly for my benefit, but I had an uncomfortable suspicion that they would all enjoy themselves more, free of my unwillingly restrictive presence. Alone in the deserted garden, I tried to concentrate on the papers and ignore irrational fears of traffic congestion, accidents and other kinds of disaster, but the hours passed very slowly and I did not appreciate my freedom.

When they returned they were eager to regale me with full details of their outing—of the farm they had stopped at, where there were baby piglets; and how a week-old calf had nuzzled Anna's hand. Simon was as flushed and laughing as the children. I remembered with a pang of jealousy that it had been the same at the zoo, despite the pouring rain on that occasion.

We spent the whole of bank holiday in the garden. Simon brought out a croquet set and had endless games with the children, followed by a make-shift cricket match which I was called on to umpire. That evening we were all aware of having been in the sun, and despite the filter cream I had carefully insisted on, Anna's fair skin was red and burning.

Then it was Tuesday and Simon left us, still at the breakfast table, to return to work.

'What shall we do today?' Paul demanded, digging into the marmalade.

'Well, there's the pool, the croquet, and cricket—'

But that was too easy. 'We did all that yesterday.'

I sighed. That was what I'd been afraid of.'

'Then how about taking Anna riding this morning?'

The boys groaned but Anna clapped her hands delightedly.

'You two can have a go as well if you like,' I

wheedled, but they were not impressed. However, we dug out Anna's trews and riding hat, thoughtfully packed by Cathy, and walked round to the stables, where Anna was greeted with enthusiasm. Of course she could have a ride, but although old Patch was still there, Anna was now too big for him. He was ceremoniously visited and fed with pieces of apple. Then Anna had her ride while her brothers, thawing slightly, peered into the dim stables and helped to fill the mangers with clean hay.

The phone was ringing as we came in the front door at lunch time and I caught it up to find it was Sally.

'How goes it, Cherry? On your knees?'

'Just about!'

'I wondered if you'd like to send them round to tea this afternoon?'

'Are you sure it's not too much trouble?'

'Of course not. They used to play quite amicably with the twins, so all should be well. And I was going to suggest that one day— perhaps Thursday—we could all pile into the station wagon and take a picnic to the woods.'

'What would I do without you?' I asked gratefully.

So, with Sally's help, the long week slowly passed. My relationship with the children did not noticeably improve. Their constant bickering lacerated my nerves. Once I lost my temper and shouted back at them, and they stared at me open-mouthed. No doubt Mummy never did that. It was futile, I told myself, to be jealous of children, but that was at the root of it. I couldn't relax and be natural with them, and of course they knew it. I was miserably conscious of Simon's exasperation and that just made things worse.

'They don't like me,' I said dejectedly one evening as I was brushing my hair at the dressing-table.

'Nonsense. It's just that you don't know how to treat them. And, being children, they naturally take advantage of the fact.'

'I might stand a chance of winning over Paul and Anna if it weren't for James. But they follow his lead and I think he really hates me.'

'How could he possibly hate you?' Simon demanded impatiently. 'Has he ever given you any real reason to believe that?'

'It's just the way he looks at me. He's probably jealous for Cathy; I suppose you can't blame him.'

'We can hardly punish him just for looking, but if he's ever rude or disobedient, of course he'll be dealt with.'

'I don't want him "dealt with",' I said flatly. 'I just want—oh, I don't know.' I dropped the brush with a clatter on to the dressing-table. 'I wish I could love them for you, Simon.'

'Don't worry about that, Cathy loves them enough for everyone. Anyway, tomorrow's their last day. I'm sorry the week has been such a trial.'

'Oh, it's not been too bad,' I said hastily, afraid to admit the extent of my despair. 'I suppose I'm just tired.'

I slipped off my dressing gown and climbed into bed and after a moment Simon got in beside me and switched off the light. We lay for a while side by side, while I prayed for a touch of his hand or a word of comfort. But he only said, 'Good night, then' and turned on his side away from me. The hot, slow tears slid down my cheeks, salty on my lips.

'Good night,' I whispered.

The next day was an extension of my misery. The children, ready-packed, couldn't settle to anything. Twice James and Paul started fighting and had to be separated. Anna slipped on the wet grass by the paddling pool and her case had to be unpacked to extract dry clothes for her. By the time Simon came home, we were all bored and irritable.

During the children's stay we had had our evening meal altogether in the 'supper room.' This last meal of the visit was supposed to be a special occasion, but it didn't turn out like that.

For a while we ate in silence, then, making an effort, Simon remarked, 'This time tomorrow you'll be home. Have you enjoyed your holiday?'

The answering mumble was hard to distinguish. Anna, elbow propped on the table, waved her fork backwards and forwards in the way I had been trying to stop for the last week.

'Daddy, why are you living here with Cherry, when we're up in Ripon with Mummy? Aren't you our proper Daddy any more?'

In the silence that followed I was aware only of the sound of my own breathing, harsh and grating. Then Simon said flatly. 'Of course I'm still your proper Daddy. Nothing can change that. But now that Cherry and I are married—'

'But I don't see why you married her. Don't you love Mummy any more?'

'No,' James answered, before Simon could reply. 'Cherry came and made him love her instead!'

I could bear no more. 'That's not true, James! Daddy and Mummy had stopped really loving each other long before Daddy met me!' Even to my own ears, that statement seemed totally the wrong thing to tell children. I turned wildly to Simon. 'You explain to them! Make them understand!'

'We do understand,' said James stolidly. 'You don't like children, so you made Daddy stop loving us all and live here with you in our house.'

I stared at him helplessly, trying to think of a way to defend myself, but my eyes were wrenched from his face by Simon's hand smashing down on the table.

'Now that's quite enough! James, you've no

right to speak like that to Cherry. She's done nothing to hurt you in any way. Apologize to her at once!'

The boy's face was frightened but obstinate. 'I can't, because I'm not sorry!'

'In that case we'll have to make you sorry. Go to your room!' Simon's voice was shaking. Whitefaced, James went out.

'Oh Simon, no!' I whispered, stricken by the child's expression. 'Go after him, please! Convince him that you still love him!'

'Kindly allow me to deal with my own children, Cherry,' said Simon tightly. I gasped. My own. Not yours. Hands off.

Anna burst into tears and even Paul's round, cherubic face was woebegone.

'Please may I get down?' he whispeted, his eyes on his plate. Simon nodded silently and Paul fled, closely followed by Anna.

'Well,' Simon said heavily into the stillness. 'you wanted me to stick up for you, didn't you?'

'Not like that. Simon, he's only a child!'

He gave a bark of laughter. 'That's what I've been trying to tell you. But this time he needs to be punished; he was deliberately trying to hurt you.'

'Only because he feels I've hurt him—all of them. Now he'll never forgive me.'

The door opened and Anna's wide, tear-stained eyes regarded us fearfully. 'James is being sick!' she announced awesomely.

I pushed back my chair but Simon snapped, 'Sit down!' and then, to Anna, 'Is he in the bathroom?' She nodded.

'All right. Tell him to go to bed when he's finished.'

I stared at him in horror. 'Simon, that child needs comforting!'

'Nonsense. It's probably only a mouthful or two he's brought up out of sheer rage.'

'I'm sorry, but I'm going to him.' I didn't look at his face as I ran out of the room and up the stairs. I met James coming out of the bathroom, one hand against the wall to support himself. His face had a greenish tinge and his small brow was beaded with sweat. This was no make-believe sickness.

'Do you feel better now, darling?' The endearment was instinctive, unnoticed by either of us.

He shook his head. 'I've still got a tummy-ache. I've had it all day.'

'Why didn't you tell me?'

His lips trembled. 'I didn't think you'd care.'

I gathered him into my arms, full of contrition. 'Of course I care. Now come along and I'll help you get into bed. Paul—' to our round-eyed audience— 'go down and ask Mrs. Charles to fill a hot-water bottle for James.'

In his room, James stood woodenly and allowed me to undress him and put on his pyjamas. I helped him into bed and tucked the hot-water bottle in beside him.

'Does that help?'

It might have been my unexpected tenderness that made his eyes fill. 'I want my Mummy,' he said.

I sat on the bed and gently stroked his head. 'Paul, have your bath now and get into bed as quietly as you can so as not to disturb James. And call me if he's sick again.'

Paul nodded importantly. I saw Anna into bed and went slowly back downstairs. Simon was in the sitting room. He had switched on the television and didn't look up as I went in. I kept my eyes on the screen. Incredibly our positions were now reversed. I was on the children's side against him. And he'd only reacted because I'd been complaining of James's attitude towards me.

'Simon—'

'Cherry!' Paul's voice over the bannisters sent me running into the hall. 'James has been sick again!'

'All right, I'm coming.'

At least he needed me, even if his father didn't. The cold phrase, *my own children*, continued to ring in my ears, proof of exclusion where before I had wanted no part of ownership.

Twice more during the evening I was called upstairs to James. When I returned to the sitting room the last time I said to Simon, 'I'm worried about him. He shouldn't have to face that long journey tomorrow.'

'Nonsense,' Simon said abruptly. 'It's possible for him to make himself sick, you know. He's done it before. It's a way of getting attention—making you feel guilty. He'll be all right in the morning, you'll see.'

Incredibly enough he was right. I was not used to a child's ability to shake off sickness, and it was little short of miraculous to me that, apart from a certain paleness, James seemed his old self the next morning. To my anxious inquiries he replied merely that he was 'all right' and yes, he wanted to go home as arranged.

So our silent little party piled into the car and set off once more for King's Cross. The children's escort was waiting, and I warned her to keep an eye on James. Then, with dutiful kisses all round, we said good-bye and they went through the barrier onto the platform. Simon and I were alone. I tried to think of something to say but he had already told me not to interfere. In any case, he forestalled me.

'I don't know about you, but I could do with some cheerful company after all that. Let's call on Tom and Helen on the off chance of finding them in.'

My heart sank. 'I–I'd really rather go straight home, Simon. I'm a bit limp—not in the mood for visiting.'

'You'll be all the better for a couple of hours with them.'

I doubted it but I was out of luck. They were

indeed at home and greeted us with pleasure.

'Stay for a meal! We'd love you to! We've nothing on this evening. So you've had the children with you. How were they?'

'Diabolical!' said Simon heavily, slumping into a chair. 'Cheery stipulates no children, and my God, I think she's got something after all. Give me a week of conferences any day.'

I caught Helen's quick, interested glance and felt betrayed. Simon should have appreciated that our discussion about children was something private to us, but after the last week we seemed poles apart. I sat apathetically while Helen bustled around producing a delectable sponge cake and a tray of tea things. It was too much effort to rouse myself to light conversation. All I wanted was oblivion.

Simon and Tom sat and talked quietly between themselves and I let Helen's words rattle meaninglessly against my ears, knowing but almost uncaring that the gulf between Simon and me had not escaped her. And we'd been married only two months. She had generously allowed us six. Was this, I wondered morosely, how it had been with Cathy? Did Simon always get bored so quickly?

At about six o'clock he and Tom left in search of what Tom called 'a jar.'

'We won't see them again for some time,' Helen commented. 'So sit back and tell Auntie

Helen what's wrong. Was I right, or were you?'

'About what?' I fenced.

'Oh come on, now! You can hardly pretend nothing's the matter when you sit there politely avoiding each other's eyes for a couple of hours.'

Again I was aware of resentment at her bland assumption of the right to question me. I said a little stiffly, 'There's nothing wrong between Simon and me, but there was trouble last night with James. That's what's upsetting us.'

'Well, it's not the end of the world. We're always having trouble with our kids.'

But at least, I thought numbly, they belong to both of you. Helen's eyes were assessingly on my face.

'And it's true you don't want any of your own?'

'Quite true,' I said numbly. After Simon's comment there was no point in denying it.

'Well, I suppose you know what you're doing, but Simon's always been very fond of children and he never got much of a look-in with the other lot. Seems a shame he should miss out twice.'

I said in a high voice, 'Do you think we could change the subject, Helen? I've had enough of children for the moment. Tell me what you've been doing since we last saw you.'

Diverted of necessity from her consuming interest in the state of our marriage, she talked happily enough about the holiday they had just spent in Corsica, about a new car Tom was thinking of buying, and various other safe topics. At eight o'clock I went with her to the kitchen and watched her start to prepare the meal. My ears were now permanently straining for the men's return, but it was nine before I was rewarded. I ran back to the drawing room as they came in the door.

'Here he is, Cherry, all safe and sound!' Tom said heartily. 'Helen in the kitchen? I've brought her back a bottle of wine.' He went through to find her.

Simon said softly, 'Come here.' I didn't need telling twice. He caught me against him, his face in my hair. 'Oh Cherry, you seemed so far away!'

'No, no I wasn't.' I pressed against him. He moved his head sharply and his mouth found mine. Tom's voice behind us said, 'Don't mind me—I'm blind!' Simon took him at his word and his arms didn't slacken. It was the most wonderful kiss we had ever shared, the first time there had been no holding back. When it was over he said unevenly, 'That's very much better. Sweetheart, I know I've been like a bear with a sore head. Will you forgive me?'

'It wasn't easy for any of us,' I said gently. 'It'll be better next time.'

He looked at me quickly. 'You mean you'll have them again? After all this?'

'Oh darling, you couldn't have thought that

I wouldn't!'

'What frightened me was that they seemed to come between us. That shouldn't have been possible.'

'It won't be, again.'

There was an expression in his eyes that I hadn't seen there before, and it filled me with a wild, singing joy. He said softly. 'Oh Cherry—' but before he could finish, Helen's voice called gaily, 'I'm coming in! All clear?' and we reluctantly moved apart. I wondered painfully if he had, at last, been going to say that he loved me. It was, incredibly enough, a subject which had never been raised since the night he asked me to marry him—and then I hadn't believed him. But despite the interruption I was suddenly unbearably happy. To be close to him again after the miseries of the last few days was the only thing that mattered. I turned to Helen with a radiant smile. Her eyes went from me to Simon.

'Wow!' she said.

It was a gay meal, all the tensions dissolved. It even seemed possible that Helen and I could come to a mutual understanding. We sat a long time over the coffee, talking easily about politics and conservation and a hundred other things. And beneath the table Simon's hand tightly held mine.

'You must come and visit us soon,' I said confidently as we were leaving. We drove home with dreamy music on the car radio and

Simon's arm round my shoulders. I was tired and supremely happy. And when we reached home we would have the house to ourselves. Of course the children would come again, but at the moment there was a comfortable time lapse separating us from their next visit. Please God, when they did come, Simon and I would be very much more sure of each other and they would present no threat.

The car turned into the driveway. I pushed the children out of my mind and gave all my attention to my husband.

CHAPTER SIX

When Simon told me, about ten days later, that he would be attending a dinner in town the following week, it seemed a good opportunity to contact Sue and Lucy and invite them out for a meal. It would even be an advantage not to have Simon with us, since we could indulge in the kind of gossip that used to sustain us when we shared the flat together.

It was Sue who answered the phone. 'Cherry! I was afraid you'd struck us off your visiting list!'

'I know it's been some time—I'm sorry. How are things?'

'Much the same as ever. What about you?'

'Oh, fine—wonderful!' I amended, not sure

that 'fine' was a strong enough recommendation for married bliss. 'I was wondering if you and Lucy could come and have dinner with me on Friday next week? Simon has some boring old dinner in town and it would give us a chance to get talked up-to-date.'

'We'd love to. How do we get there?'

'If you can get the train to Cheston I'll meet you at the station. There's one that leaves Waterloo at five-thirty-five, if you could manage that.'

'We'll be on it. It'll be lovely to see you again.'

Cheston in summer was green and gold. After living most of my life in the north, I could still not accept without wonder the lushness of trees and plants in these southern counties. It was a physical pleasure to feast my eyes on the gracious trees which lined every road, and the riot of colour in the carefully-tended gardens. I revelled in it all again that evening, as I walked slowly home from the station with Lucy and Sue. The house looked mellow and gracious in the evening sunlight and although I still couldn't think of it as mine, I accepted my friends' exclamations of admiration on Simon's behalf.

We had dinner with the dining room windows open to the warm night air and hosts of tiny winged insects circled the light. It was very pleasant to sit leisurely over coffee after an enjoyable meal, our talk more desultory now that all the main things had been said.

'And you really are happy, Cherry?' Lucy inquired suddenly.

'Yes, really. Didn't you expect me to be?'

'I'm not sure. It was all so headlong, somehow.'

I laughed. 'We don't all go around together for a couple of years while we make up our minds!'

'You're right, of course. I think if I really loved Tim, I'd have married him ages ago. It's just a question of marking time till something, better turns up!' she added outrageously.

'What about your new flat-mate? Do you get on well with her?'

'So-so. She keeps to herself and no information is ever volunteered about her private life, nor is she really interested in ours. Quite a change from you! She has what used to be known as a 'gentleman friend' who calls for her two evenings a week and every Saturday, but we know nothing whatever about him. Most galling! We've decided he must be someone well-known, a film star or M.P. or someone, with a family in the background. Pure speculation, of course, just to liven things up a bit! Once I "happened" to be downstairs when he called,' but it didn't do me any good. For one thing, he never gets out of the car— just sits and toots—and for another, he was wearing dark glasses.'

'Most mysterious!' I agreed.

'Except,' said Lucy drily, 'that it happened to be a brilliantly sunny afternoon!'

We were still laughing when the telephone sounded in the hall.

'I'd better answer it, if you'll excuse me. I heard Mrs. Charles go upstairs.'

I hurried out, leaving the dining room door ajar.

'Could I speak to Mr. Slade, please?' It was a woman's voice, low and vibrant.

'I'm sorry, he isn't in this evening. Can I take a message?'

There was a fractional pause. 'To whom am I speaking?'

'This is Mrs. Slade.'

'*Mrs.* Slade?' The surprise in the voice resounded along the wire. She said incredulously, 'Cathy?'

My hand tightened on the receiver. 'No, Cherry. Who is speaking, please?'

There was another pause and then a low laugh. 'Well, well! In that case my call seems somewhat superfluous! Just tell him, would you, that Rona phoned? There's no message. I'm sorry to have troubled you, Mrs. Slade.'

The phone clicked in my ear. I went on holding it, waiting for my breath to steady, the heat to leave my face. The words repeated themselves in my head like a recorded message. Who was she, and what had she wanted with Simon? I'd never heard him speak of anyone called Rona, but since she'd been

99

surprised to think I might be Cathy, it must be someone he'd met since their separation.

Since I couldn't go on standing in the hall all night, I finally replaced the receiver, wiped my sticky palms on my handkerchief and went back into the dining room. Sue said quickly, 'There's nothing wrong, is there?'

'No, nothing. Just someone for Simon. Would anyone like some more coffee?'

But the sparkle had gone out of the evening—I could only give them half my attention. Eventually Sue said, 'I hate to mention it, but if we're to catch the ten-thirty we ought to be making a move.'

'I'll phone for a taxi,' I said. They were suddenly very dear to me, concerned and dependable. I almost wished I'd told them about the call—we could have laughed about it and diminished its impact, and perhaps that would have dispelled the heavy feeling inside me. The sound of the taxi drawing up reached us from outside.

'You will come again, won't you? Soon?'

'If we're asked!' dimpled Lucy. 'But the next time Simon's going to be out, you come to us. He could pick you up afterwards.'

The doorbell rang.

'Let me know if you discover the identity of Mr. X!'

They were gone. I left the porch light on for Simon and closed the outer door. The house was still and restful but I was not soothed. I walked back into the dining room to close the windows. Mrs. Charles would clear away the coffee things in the morning. It was very luxurious, I told myself, to have someone to wash the dishes, but I suddenly decided to do them myself, now. I didn't want to lie awake waiting for Simon. and wondering about the mysterious Rona.

I stacked the cups and saucers, the cream jug and coffee pot onto the little tray and carried it precariously through to the kitchen. The room was warm and quiet, a faint suggestion of rich wine sauce hung on the still air. The preparation for this meal had occasioned another slight breach with Mrs. Charles, since I had insisted on doing the cooking myself.

'But Mrs. Slade always left the cooking to me!' she declared, quite offended. 'She used to say she had complete faith in me!'

'But I happen to enjoy cooking, Mrs. Charles. I leave the day to day meals to you and they're always delicious, but I like doing special recipes myself.'

She refused to accept reason. 'But Mrs. Slade always—'

My patience had snapped. 'I'm Mrs. Slade now, and I'm rather tired of continually hearing how my cousin ran this house. I intend to do it my way and as long as that's quite clear everything should go smoothly.'

I remembered the contretemps now, as I

tied an apron over my dress and ran water into the bowl. I hated unpleasantness, but it was obviously necessary to take a firm hand with Mrs. Charles or she would continue to run the house as she had when Simon was alone.

Slowly and carefully I immersed the fragile china, rinsed it and put it on the draining board. It didn't take long. I looked round for something else to wash, but the rest of the dishes were clean and stacked on the counter, waiting to be put away with the coffee service in the morning. Regretfully I hung up the apron again, dried the cups and saucers and put them with the other plates.

The sitting room was dappled with moonlit shadows from the uncurtained windows, dancing as the trees outside moved faintly in the merest suggestion of a breeze. Come home, Simon, and tell me how silly I'm being! I sighed, pulled the door to behind me and went slowly upstairs, followed by the strong, sweet perfume from the bowl of roses on the hall table.

In spite of myself, I fell asleep over my book. I woke with a start to hear the front door beneath me being closed, and glanced at the bedside clock. It was twelve-thirty. Simon came quietly into the room in his shirt sleeves, his jacket slung over his shoulder. He looked surprised to see me awake.

'Hello, love. How did the evening go?'

'Fine, thank you. How was yours?'

He grimaced. 'Hot and sticky and boring as hell! Too much to eat and drink and not much chance of a contract at the end of it, in my opinion. I'm going to have a shower. How are the ex-guardian angels? Found anyone else to tuck under their joint wing?'

'They've another girl in with them, yes, but I don't know that she fits in all that well.' Who's Rona? I couldn't ask him now, with his mind on the shower. When he came back—but it must be tonight or I shouldn't be able to sleep. He extracted his pyjamas from under the pillow and went through to the bathroom, leaving the door ajar.

'By the way, we're moving offices. The lease is up or something. They're having the devil of a job finding somewhere suitable, near enough to the factory and not too far from the Exchange.'

The rush of water drowned any reply I might have made. I lay tense, waiting for him.

'If the worst comes to the worst I might have to work at home for a while,' he continued when he could make himself heard again. 'But that's not an ideal situation by any means. What's more, some men from the Chicago office are due over soon. It'll be a fine thing if we can't accommodate them.'

He reappeared in the doorway, towelling his hair.

'That's better! Now I feel human again—

and very tired. What time is it?'

'Nearly one.'

'No wonder!' He tossed the towel back into the bathroom, where it doubtless landed on the floor. I had to ask him while I could still see his face. I said—and to my surprise my voice sounded light and casual—

'By the way, there was a phone call for you this evening. A lady with a very sexy voice. Rona someone.'

He stopped abruptly halfway across the room. 'Rona?' he echoed sharply, and then, half under his breath. 'My God!'

'Who is she?' I asked, and there was only the smallest tremor. I don't think he noticed it.

'Someone I knew in Kenya.'

It fell into place. 'When,' I suggested brittlely, 'you were leading your less-than-monastic life?'

He threw me a glance, darkly unreadable. 'That's right. What did she want?'

'You, I imagine. She seemed mightily surprised when she heard who I was. She said—' unintentionally my voice took on the mocking intonation—' "In that case my call is superfluous!" '

'And what do you suppose she meant by that?'

'Perhaps,' I said unforgivably, out of intense jealousy, 'she was about to offer her services again.'

'Cherry!' He stared at me whitely.

I licked my lips. 'I'm sorry, darling, but I've been consumed with jealousy all evening.' My deliberate over-emphasis was designed to gloss over the truth of what I said, and I think it worked, because he looked at me curiously for a moment before saying briskly,

'You needn't have been. It was over before we met.' Which was what he'd said about Cathy.

'Over? Or just postponed? Perhaps she had expected to take up the reins again when she got back to this country.'

He didn't speak. Couldn't he see how desperately I needed reassurance, which his curt dismissal of the matter had done nothing to supply?

'You did have an affair with her?' I pursued, unable to stop twisting the knife.

'Yes. I wasn't trying to hide anything. It just didn't seem important.'

Irony indeed. He got into bed and reached up to switch off the light. In the sudden darkness I tensed, waiting for his next move. After a moment he added, 'As a matter of fact, I'd forgotten all about her.'

'She hasn't forgotten you.'

'No. You were right, she did say she'd get in touch when she got back to England. Actually she has some books of mine. I suppose she wanted to return them.'

I said with difficulty, 'Did you love her'?'

'No!' His voice was sharp.

'Tell me about her.'

'Why? Whatever's the point?'

His truculent tone annoyed me. Surely I didn't have to give reasons for wanting to know about woman my husband had gone to bed with. If only he would take me in his arms and swear that it was unimportant—above all, that it was me he loved. But instead, guilt had put him on the defensive.

I forced my voice to lightness. 'Just academic interest.'

After a moment be said tightly, 'There's not much to tell. She worked at the hotel where I lived. She was glamorous and—well, yes, sexy—you were right about that, too. I was pretty miserable, still drinking too much, and so on. She was good company—amusing, intelligent. I liked her.'

'How long did it go on?'

'Quite a while, on and off. I was moving about the country a lot, but Nairobi was my base.'

'Was she in love with you?'

'I shouldn't think so. The subject never came up.' That I could believe. 'It was a purely physical thing,' he added. 'Next question?'

'How old was she?'

'Late twenties, probably. Old enough to know what she was doing, anyway. Don't make me out a seducer, Cherry, it was a mutual arrangement. I'm not sure the initial move didn't come from her.'

I surprised myself with a feeling of pity for the unknown Rona. Of course she had loved him—she probably still did. 'You didn't write to her?' I persisted.

'Once, just to say I'd arrived. And by the time her reply came I'd met you.'

'No wonder it was a shock to find you'd married again. After all, that was only six months ago.'

'Yes. Have I satisfied your academic interest now? Because I'm absolutely exhausted and I must be up at seven to be in time for a meeting. Forget about her. I told you it's all over.'

He leaned over and kissed me briefly. Perhaps if I'd been less flippant, let him know how deeply I felt about it, he might have made more effort to comfort me. But my stupid pride continually stopped me from admitting how much he meant to me until I was more certain of him. And now, I thought desolately, I was less sure than ever. It was a long time before I fell asleep.

*   *   *

She came the next day. I think I almost expected her. Certainly the small white car which cruised past so slowly immediately attracted my attention. At the end of the road it turned, as I had known it would, and drove slowly back again. It stopped a little beyond our gate. I waited, standing rigidly in the centre of the sitting room. I heard a car door slam, and then again, as though she had got something out of the back. Then she approached the gate, a tall, slim figure with an armful of books. She hesitated, staring up at the house, and I kept well back from the window. Then she came quickly up the path. I tensed, waiting for the bell to ring. But it didn't, and a moment later I heard her footsteps on the path again. I ran into the hall and flung the door open. The pile of books was stacked neatly on the porch and she was halfway down the path. She spun round and for a moment we stared at each other. Then she said quickly, 'I'm sorry, I didn't intend to disturb you. I've left some books for your husband.'

'You're Rona, aren't you?'

'And you're Cherry.'

'Would you like to come in for a moment? Simon isn't here.'

'Oh no, no thank you. I just—I mean, I should have posted them, but the postage these days—'

'Please come in. I can at least give you a cup of tea.'

Still she hesitated. 'Mrs. Slade—'

'It's all right.' I said gently. 'I know.'

She let her breath out in a little sigh and came slowly back up the path. 'I honestly didn't mean you to see me. I just wanted—to see where he lived.

I stood to one side and she came into the hall. I put my head around the kitchen door. 'Mrs. Charles, I have a visitor. Would you bring tea to the sitting-room, please?'

Then we were together, Rona and I, frankly sizing each other up. Her face was oval and finely boned, and there were smudgy purple shadows around her eyes. It was my guess that last night she had slept no better than I had.

'Do sit down.' I was asking myself whatever had possessed me to force this confrontation and she must have been wondering the same thing. She sat on the edge of a chair, looking around the pleasant, flower-filled room. This time yesterday, we hadn't known of each other's existence.

'Mrs. Slade—'

'Cherry.'

'I'm sorry I was so foul on the phone. It was such a shock—'

'I understand.'

'You've no cause to worry, of course. On his side there was nothing. No doubt he told you that. It was just a general sort of need, and I was there at the time. That's all.'

'And on your side?'

She met my eyes frankly. 'I think you know the answer to that. I was hoping that by now he'd have had time to get over Cathy.' She stopped suddenly, embarrassment flooding over her face, and in the pause that followed Mrs. Charles came in with the tea tray.

When we were alone again I said quietly, 'Cathy's my cousin. It hasn't been easy for me, either.' I picked up the silver teapot, noting with detachment that my hand was shaking.

'Your cousin? So he knew you all along?'

'Only as a little bridesmaid. I'm six years younger than she is. I met him quite by chance one evening soon after he'd got back. We arranged to meet to exchange news—and that was it.'

'It must have been very quick.'

'Yes. Yes, it was.' I passed her a teacup. Her hand was trembling as much as mine. This wasn't the Rona I'd imagined after the phone call. Rather to my discomfort I found that I liked her, that under different circumstances we could have been friends.

She said suddenly, 'You won't blame Simon for my stupidity, will you? Obviously I should never have come here. Even if I hadn't known he'd married it would have been a long shot. He had no idea how I felt, I'm sure of that. If he considered the matter at all, he no doubt imagined I was in the habit of dishing out comfort to the troops.' She looked up. 'What will you tell him?'

'Only that you returned the books.'

'Thank you.' She put her cup down abruptly and stood up. 'I think I'd better go. Thank you for being so understanding.'

I stood at the door watching her go down the path, but she didn't turn round. There but for the grace of God—

I brought the books in from the porch and put them on the hall table. Simon saw them as soon as he came in.

'Rona brought them,' I said.

He stared at me. 'She came here?'

'Yes. We had a cup of tea.'

'Well, I'm damned! Of all the nerve—coming here and confronting my wife!'

I said sharply, 'It wasn't like that at all. She'd intended to leave them in the porch but I happened to see her, so I—asked her in.'

'Isn't that carrying 'academic interest' a little too far?'

'I don't think so. I liked her.'

'I'm so glad! What did you find to talk about?'

'You, mainly.'

'Now look, I've already—'

'It's all right. She corroborated what you said.'

He turned sharply, his eyes raking my face. 'Was it necessary to check?'

'Oh darling no!' I went to him quickly, laying my hand on his arm. 'That wasn't what I meant at all.'

He stared into my face for a moment. 'I suppose I can at least be grateful you haven't a jealous nature!'

'But I have! I told you before—'

'Consumed with jealousy,' I'd said. He hadn't believed me, of course.

He smiled briefly and turned away. 'Let's forget it, shall we? I could use a drink.'

'But Simon—'

'Yes?'

'Nothing,' I said wistfully.

CHAPTER SEVEN

Slowly June passed, and I fought a losing battle with the doubts and uncertainties which afflicted me. Our marriage was not a restful thing: we could never wholly relax with each other. Too many shadows hovered on the outskirts: Cathy and the children, my parents' continuing displeasure, even Rona. I tortured myself by wondering whether, if Simon had been in when she phoned, he would have arranged to see her again. Or even have wanted to. The curtain of restraint, lifted so briefly the evening at the Edwardses', was again between us, even during our love-making. Fight it as I would, an insidious air of disillusion was creeping into our marriage, and it terrified me.

To counteract it, I was unnaturally bright, plundering the garden to fill every corner of the house with gaily coloured flowers, poring for hours over recipes to find new and exciting dishes for dinner, and spending long hours in front of the mirror upstairs trying out new make-up, new hairstyles, new perfume, which would somehow miraculously make me irresistible. As a result, all this frantic effort had the opposite effect: I became strained and irritable, and Simon retreated still further.

At the beginning of July he had to attend an evening conference in town and, as promised, I phoned Sue and Lucy. Dinner at the flat would be just like old times, since Vera, their flat-mate, was away on holiday.

'You look tired, Cherry,' Sue said critically as we sat with our sherry before dinner.

'Not very complimentary!' I said in light rebuke. 'And you haven't even mentioned my tan!'

'Underneath it you're pale, and there are shadows under your eyes. You look as though you could do with a holiday.'

'Simon can't get away till September this year, and of course we had a week in April. Still, life's one long holiday, with Mrs. Charles to do all the work!'

'Is it?' Sue's eyes were probing and my defences crumbled.

'No, as a matter of fact it isn't.'

'Would it help to talk about it?'

'There's nothing to say, that's the trouble. Nothing you could put your finger on. But Simon and I seem to be growing further and further apart.'

'In what way?'

'Oh, I don't know. Nothing is ever spontaneous. We stop and think before we say anything, weighing our words. Some subjects are completely taboo—principally the children. There was a ghastly scene with them the last time they were with us, and I know it's still on Simon's mind. What's more, he blames me for it.'

'What happened?'

'Oh, I'd been complaining that James didn't like me, so when he was a bit outspoken that evening Simon over-reacted. And since it happened at bed time, and they went home the next day, it was never put right. To make things even worse, James was sick that night. Nerves, I suppose. Simon insisted he was putting it on, but I don't think so. He's a quiet, serious child, and his parents splitting up obviously had much more effect on him than on the others, probably because he's older.'

'But that's the only thing you can really tie down as a reason for friction?'

'More or less.'

Lucy said quietly, 'We were rather worried about that phone call the night we came for dinner.'

'That was unpleasant at the time but I think it's sorted itself out now. It was from a girl Simon knew in Africa. She'd just arrived back herself, and it was a shock to find he was married.'

Lucy said gently, 'We're not trying to pry, you know. It's just that we're worried about you and you seem rather cut off down there in Surrey. I don't suppose you could confide in your new neighbours, and your parents are too far away—so if there's anything we can do, just say so.'

'Bless you, Lucy, but I don't honestly think there is. And please don't think I'm criticizing Simon. He's never done anything I could take exception to. I suppose,' I added after a minute, 'the trouble has always been that I love him too much. Considerably more than he's prepared—or perhaps even able—to love me.'

'He'd no right to ask you to marry him!' Lucy said violently. 'It was incredibly selfish!'

'Not really.' I had to defend him, even against myself. 'You see, he has no idea how deeply I feel about him.' I realized as I spoke that I was echoing Rona's words. It certainly seemed that Simon had a blind spot where women were concerned, but I wasn't prepared to admit Lucy's suggestion that selfishness lay behind it. He was basically too considerate to be accused of that.

'It's simply a matter of pride,' I went on. 'There's no point in embarrassing him with protestations he can't reciprocate, so he probably feels we're pretty evenly matched. Oh, we have our good moments, of course—

when everything's wonderful. Then for some reason the barriers come crashing down again, and I'm firmly on the outside.'

'Do you regret having married him?' Sue asked bluntly.

'Good heavens, no! I love him—I could never be happy with anyone else. Sorry, I must have been piling on the agony, rather, but you did ask. Anyway, that's quite enough about me. Have you found out anything more about Vera's mysterious lover?'

Lucy laughed. 'Oh, an awful anticlimax! He's pale and thin, with a prominent Adam's apple, and his name is Fred!'

'To be fair,' Sue corrected, 'it's Frederick. That's what Vera always calls him, but admittedly he looks more like a Fred!'

The conversation remained in this lighter vein for the rest of the evening but, as Simon's car pulled up outside, Lucy said quickly,

'You know we're with you, don't you one hundred percent? If ever you need to talk to anyone, we're always here.'

'Pleasant hen party?' Simon inquired, turning the car in a wide circle and heading for home.

'Very pleasant. I miss them, even though I have Sally and Sylvia. 'How did the conference go?'

'Everyone's in a bit of a sweat about this lease business. We have to be out by the end of the month and they still haven't found

116

alternative accommodation. They're talking now about taking over some existing buildings and converting them, but this will need planning permission and could take an age. In the meantime the Yanks' visit is looming ever nearer. God knows what we're going to do with them.'

I leaned my head back and closed my eyes, tensing my body against every twist and turn of the car.

'I think I'll start bringing my stuff home, bit by bit. I don't want it mislaid in the general hiatus, and if the worst comes to the worst I could work from home—perhaps turn the guest room into a temporary office.'

His voice came and went like waves in my sleepy brain, merging with the rushing of the car's movement.

'Of course, it would mean that my American would have to come too. We've each been allotted one to look after, our opposite number, so to speak. Though how we're to get any work done with no secretaries on hand, Lord only knows and we can hardly expect one to come traipsing out to us every day.'

'I could do it,' I said drowsily.

'What?' I could tell from the clarity of his voice that his head had turned towards me.

'I used to be a secretary, remember.'

'Now why didn't I think of that! How very clever of you, my love!'

'I'd expect a good rate of pay, mind!' I said

with a laugh.

'I don't see why you shouldn't be taken on as a temporary. I could easily swipe a typewriter for you. That would certainly simplify matters.'

The following weekend—under Simon's direction—he, Mrs. Charles and I struggled to prepare the guest room for its *volte face*. There was just room for the bed in the boys' room, but the wardrobe was too cumbersome to move. Since half of it was filled with shelves it was decided to make use of it as it was, and once the dressing table mirror was removed it made quite an adequate desk. At last, Simon stood back and surveyed the transformation with satisfaction.

'That'll do admirably. The telephone engineer will be here on Monday to put in an extension, and I've told Smithers I could do with an extra desk and a typewriter. They cleared your appointment, by the way. Since we're not sure how much there'll be for you to do, you'll be paid on an hourly basis, which I think is usual for temps anyway. So, against all odds, it looks as though we'll be ready for action when the Americans arrive after all. Though, of course, with temporary offices scattered all over London, it will still have complications. Still, the old man refused point-blank to postpone their visit and, admittedly, it would be difficult—with all the arrangements made. Incidentally, there'll be a reception for them on Thursday evening. Drinks at the Carlton, wives included.'

'But no dinner?'

'Only for the select few, and I'm afraid we don't qualify. Still, we can go on elsewhere for a meal. We haven't eaten out together since Paris.'

Which, I reflected pleasurably, would be very much more to my taste than any official function.

* * *

There were eight Americans in the party, their average age being early thirties, and Simon's protégé was tall and serious-looking, with light brown hair and steady grey eyes.

'This is Rod Cleveland, Cherry. He and I will be working together for the next few weeks.'

'Mrs. Slade.' He took my hand and bent over it with a little bow. 'It's my pleasure.'

'You'll probably see quite a lot of her,' Simon remarked. 'I've co-opted her services in the secretarial field.'

'You're lucky,' Rod Cleveland said with a smile. 'My wife wouldn't have been much help under these circumstances. She's a dietician!'

'How does she feel about being left at home all this time?'

'She's not exactly overjoyed about it. However, we're expecting an addition to the family in the fall, so she'll have plenty to do.'

'Is it the first?'

'Yes, Roderick J. Cleveland the Second—it's all arranged! It had better not be a girl! Do you have any children?'

The suddenness of the question, although entirely natural, took me by surprise. Simon cut in crisply, 'I have three by a previous marriage. Cherry and I have only been married three months.'

'Then you probably won't understand how wonderful it is for us. We've been wanting a baby for five years, and now we can hardly believe it's for real. Laurie hasn't been too well, though. We'll sure be glad when everything's safely over.' He grinned at me engagingly. 'I'm all set to become the world's most boring father, bringing out snapshots at the drop of a hat! Here's one of Laurie, to begin with!'

He fished inside his wallet and extracted a colour print of a girl standing in a garden. Her hair was blowing in the wind, and she was laughing.

'You look a little like her, Mrs. Slade.' He took it back from me, glancing down at it before he put it away. 'The hell of it is I miss her like crazy already.'

A colleague of Simon's came up with his wife, conversation became general, and eventually people began to leave. 'It's started to rain,' Simon commented. 'Give me a couple of minutes and I'll bring the car round.'

He made his *adieux* and I stood talking to some of the wives. Rod Cleveland came over. 'Mrs. Slade, I forgot to fix a time in the morning to meet your husband. Is he coming back?'

'No, he's gone for the car, but you could come down with me, and ask him.'

'Sure.'

I collected my coat, and together we left the private room and started down the main staircase to the hall, Then, as we rounded a bend, I saw them: Simon and Rona in earnest conversation by the reception desk. I stopped abruptly, clutching the bannister.

'Mrs. Slade—what happened?' His eyes followed mine and swiftly returned to my face. 'Is something wrong?'

'No. No, it's all right.'

'Shall we go on down?'

'Yes, of course.'

I knew Rod was watching me in bewildered concern, but we went together slowly down the remaining stairs. As we reached the bottom Rona quickly laid her hand over Simon's, smiled, and moved away. He turned and went quickly through the swing doors without seeing us. I said tightly, 'Don't say anything when we see him. Please.'

'Look now, I don't know who that was, but I'm quite sure—'

'But you see,' I interrupted, 'I do.'

He stared at me. 'Not his first wife?'

'No, an old friend. It's not important, really. I just didn't know she was here.'

We stood in awkward silence until Simon returned. He said jerkily. 'Hurry, Cherry, I'm not supposed to stop there.'

'Mr. Cleveland wondered what time to meet you tomorrow,' I said a little loudly.

'Sorry, Rod. I'll be there about nine. I want to label a desk and a typewriter before they get whipped off to storage. Don't know that we'll get much work done, with all that going on, but we can try. See you then.'

'See you. Good-bye, Mrs. Slade. It was great meeting you.'

I smiled briefly but I couldn't meet his eyes. Simon took my arm and hurried me out into the wet street. Now he'll tell me he saw her— or now, when we're in the car out of the rain. But he didn't. He was staring out of the windscreen, a furrow between his brows. Perhaps he had forgotten how attractive she was.

In the restaurant, I could bear it no longer. I waited until the waiter moved away with our order, then I said quietly, 'Aren't you going to tell me you met Rona?'

His eyes switched to my face and away. After a pause he said, ' "Met" is hardly the word. Saw.'

'Saw then, if you must split hairs. Weren't you going to say anything?'

122

His fingers crumbled the roll on his plate. 'There didn't seem much point in mentioning it. Please don't make a thing out of it.'

'It's you who are doing that. Surely the most natural thing would have been simply to say, 'Guess who I bumped into in the hall?' That would have proved it wasn't important, but instead you go all tense and secretive.'

His eyes glinted. 'Very well, then. "Guess who I bumped into in the hall." Is that better? Or since you like her so much, perhaps you'd have preferred me to invite her to join us for dinner?'

From being the attacker, I was thrown mercilessly onto the defensive. My eyes blurred with sudden tears.

'Simon, I—'

He sat back abruptly. 'Oh forget it, for God's sake. I saw her, we exchanged a few words, and then I went for the car. Finito—period—THE END! Would you rather I'd cut her dead? She doesn't deserve that.'

'And I don't deserve this,' I said in a whisper.

He ran his hand over his face. After a moment he said, 'I'm sorry, Cherry. Everything's getting on top of me at the moment, but you're right. It's no excuse for the way I've been behaving.'

The return of the waiter spared me from having to accept his apology. Perhaps our marriage was one of the things that was getting on top of him. Perhaps Rona had reminded him of the freedom he hadn't appreciated when he had it. Well, he knew where to find her now. Helplessly, I looked across at his tense face, the brooding eyes and stubborn chin. I love you, I love you! If only I could say it out loud!

We ate our meal in silence. The olive branch would obviously have to come from me. At last I said, 'He seems very nice, your American contact.'

Simon grunted agreement. 'One of their bright boys, I gather.' He looked up and met my eyes. I couldn't read the expression in his, but a flicker crossed his face and he reached out and squeezed my hand.

'Thanks, Cherry,' he said gently.

I wasn't quite sure why I was being thanked, for making the first move—or for accepting his explanation. Whatever the reason I gratefully returned the pressure of his hand, and an uneasy peace was restored.

The next day a van delivered the desk and an enormous typewriter, which were duly carried up to the guest room. It all looked very business-like and efficient. I practised on the typewriter most of the afternoon, familiarizing myself with its layout. It seemed much longer than three months since I had done any typing.

I saw little of Simon that weekend. Apparently, Friday had not been very productive with the moving taking place all around them, and there were one or two things that had to be discussed before Monday. Accordingly they met in London, and evidently no secretary was required.

I met Sally at the shops on Saturday morning and explained about the temporary office set-up at home.

'Good for you. It'll give you an interest.'

I raised an eyebrow. 'You think I need one?'

'Well, until the babies start coming! After all, Mrs. Charles is very capable, isn't she?'

I said stiffly, 'There won't be any babies.'

'You mean you can't have any? Oh Cherry, how awful! I—'

'I mean,' I interrupted, 'that I don't want any.'

She stared at me in astonishment. Then she said hesitantly, 'Well, it's only natural to want a little time to yourselves. But later, surely—'

'No,' I said firmly. 'Not ever.'

She digested that in silence for a moment. Then said quietly, 'Well, it's none of my business, of course, but I think you're making a mistake. I wouldn't feel properly married without a family, and Simon is so fond of the others.'

'Yes. Simon's paternal instinct, if there is such a thing, has already been gratified. He doesn't need any more.' I added in self-defence, 'I'm convinced they were part of the trouble between him and Cathy. She was tied down with them and not free to devote herself to him. I don't intend to make the same mistake.'

Sally's eyes were grave. 'You might be right about the children causing friction, but not for the reasons you suppose. Cathy was like a tiger with its cubs. No one was trusted with those children, even their own father, it seemed to us. They were very much *hers*. I honestly think he sees more of them now, when she has to allow him access, than he did when they lived together.'

Helen Edwards had said much the same thing. Still, I could hardly have a baby on approval, to see if it would work. I had never been fond of children, it was no hardship to keep to my decision.

I looked at Sally with a faint smile. 'Now, are you going to stop lecturing me and offer me a lift home? This basket is nearly breaking my arm!'

She laughed. 'Sorry. Yes. of course. The car's just along here.' We started to walk. 'What's this American of Simon's like?'

'Rather dishy, actually, but very full of his wife back home.'

'How long are they over for?'

'About six weeks, I think, but they won't be in London the whole time. The first ten days and the last, I think Simon said. In between they'll visit the Liverpool factory and also go on to Europe.'

Sally unlocked the boot of her car and we piled in our shopping. 'You must bring him round for drinks one evening. Bill was in the States some years ago so they could go into a huddle together.'

'Thanks. I don't know where he's staying—probably at the Carlton—but I should think he'll be eating with us sometimes. We can hardly pack him off hungry, especially if they've been working late.'

There was a letter from my mother waiting when I got home. I opened it with some trepidation. Mother's letters these days were brief and formal. I was still in disgrace for having cheated her of a white wedding.

'It's some time since I heard from you,' she wrote accusingly, 'but perhaps this is just as well since Beth has been staying with us for the past week. It was her first visit since your wedding, and as you will appreciate, not a very comfortable one. She says Cathy is thinking of taking a job now that Anna is at school all day. Just part-time, of course, to be home in time for the children, but the money would come in useful.'

The insinuation, apparently, was that Simon didn't provide enough. I felt a small knot of resentment. I didn't know how much he set aside for Cathy and the children. He had never mentioned it and it had certainly never occurred to me to ask. I was sure that, if anything, he would err on the generous side. It was as well, I thought, that we had enough to be comfortable, or the provision for the others could well have become yet another flashpoint. Simon had told me once that he'd received a sizable legacy on his mother's death.

He arrived home about three. 'What's the news from up north?' he asked, nodding towards the letter on the table.

He had a right to know. 'Mother says Cathy's taking a part-time job,' I said casually.

His mouth tightened. 'Why?'

'I—don't know. But now that Anna's at school—'

'Cathy isn't the career type,' Simon interrupted stiffly, 'If she's finding herself short of money, she only has to say so. I'll ask Simkins to look into it.'

Simkins was Simon's solicitor. It seemed poignant that, after all that had been between them, virtually their only contact now was through the law.

To change the subject I asked brightly, 'Did you get through everything you wanted?' I had not admitted, even to myself, the persistent niggle of suspicion that perhaps, after all, it had been Rona he had gone to meet.

'Not quite. Rod was a bit absent-minded. He's worried about his wife, apparently. He'd put a transatlantic call through and couldn't really settle down. I decided to leave before it came through, but I'll have to see him again tomorrow.'

'Is he staying at the Carlton?' Like Rona? The words I didn't say came over as clearly as those I had spoken.

'Yes. They were all booked in there.'

Did you see her? Oh, God, did you? I stood up abruptly and walked over to the window. 'Sally says we must take him round for a drink one evening.'

Simon said harshly, 'All right, she was there. Is that what you're waiting for? Of course she was there, for God's sake, she works there. It's not my fault, is it? Not that she happens to work there, nor that Rod's staying there. She said. 'Good morning, Mr. Slade' and I replied, 'Good morning, Miss Cross.' And that was positively all that passed between us. Do you require an affidavit?' He slammed his hand down on the arm of his chair. 'We're not going to go through this every time, I hope?'

'Simon, I never—'

'No, but it was in your face. Look, Cherry, you don't seem to have a very good opinion of me, so this may come as a surprise to you, but I happen to believe in the institution of marriage, despite my previous failure. I didn't go off the rails when I was married before and I won't now. What I did during the—interregnum—is neither here nor there. So could we please dispense with all the suspicions and reproachful glances, because it's getting me down. Come here.'

He raised a hand and caught mine, pulling me down on his lap. He said with a kind of rough tenderness, 'Now, will you stop being a little goose and trust me? It was only an interlude with Rona anyway, for both of us, and it's very definitely over. Okay?'

'Okay,' I said. But he was wrong about Rona.

He tipped my chin back and stared into my face. 'You are happy, aren't you? Most of the time?'

Could I even accept that qualification? There had been odd moments of delirious happiness over the last three months, but not 'most of the time.'

Uncertainty came into his eyes at my lengthening silence and I couldn't bear it. I reached up and kissed his mouth and his arms crushed me against him. Would it always be like this? I wondered miserably. I had thought being married to him would be enough. I acknowledged now that it was not, that unless I could be sure of his love I was doomed to seesaw existence. And I wasn't sure how long I could bear it.

CHAPTER EIGHT

Rod Cleveland arrived at nine o'clock on Monday morning. I ran to open the door myself, since Mrs. Charles was still busy with the breakfast dishes and Simon was going through some papers in the new 'office.'

His smile was warm and I felt a little spurt of pleasure to see him.

'Good morning, Mrs. Slade. Reporting for duty, ma'am.'

'Please come in. Simon's upstairs. I'll take you straight up.' I paused on the first step to look back at him. 'What's the news of your wife?'

His open face clouded a little. 'Not too good, I'm afraid. She seems to be having pain, which is rather worrying. The baby's not due till October.'

I said reassuringly, 'I'm sure it will be all right if she takes things quietly. Try not to worry.'

Simon had come out on the landing to greet him. Find your way all right?'

'No problem. And your charming receptionist was on the step to welcome me!'

Simon said, 'We won't be needing you for the moment, Cherry. I'll call if we do. In the meantime, if the phone goes it'll probably be for me.'

I had stopped at the stairhead, feeling like a child turned away from a party. 'Don't you even want me to answer it?'

'No, since there's no switchboard there's not much point. Come in, Rod, and I'll show you the setup.'

He turned back to the office. Rod said, 'Well, thanks again, Mrs. Slade,' and followed him. I didn't see either of them until lunch. Mrs. Charles took up some coffee at ten-thirty but I carried mine into the garden with the morning paper. If they didn't want me that was just fine, but I wasn't free to go out shopping as I would normally have done.

We had iced soup and crab salad for lunch, both of which to Mrs. Charles's tight-lipped disapproval, I had prepared myself. The French windows were open to the side lawn and the early August sun flooded warmly in. Rod was quietly appreciative of everything— the food, the room (for which Cathy deserved all the credit), even my dress, which Simon had never noticed. He and I seemed to have drawn a little closer to each other since the tense moment we had unwillingly shared on the staircase at the Carlton. I realized ruefully that he was sorry for me.

'That was just perfect, Mrs. Slade,' he declared, laying down his fork.

'Call her Cherry, for heaven's sake!' Simon said somewhat ungraciously. 'We're not as formal as all that in little old England!'

Rod smiled. 'Delighted, and we can forget the "Mr. Cleveland" too, huh?'

'Delighted!' I echoed laughingly.

Simon frowned. 'There'll probably be a letter or two this afternoon, if you'd like to come up.'

'Yes, of course.'

Accordingly, after lunch I followed him meekly up the stairs, while Rod stood aside to let me go ahead of him. It was unlike Simon to forget this courtesy and I knew the contrast between his manners and Rod's would irritate him, but that was hardly my fault. Nevertheless, he started dictating at high speed and I sensed that he wanted to disconcert me. Calmly, I refused to be disconcerted, my pencil speeding over the page as my brain clicked easily back into the well-remembered groove. The letters were mostly making appointments for Simon and Rod to visit clients the coming week. 'Confirming my telephone call of this morning—' I had not even been allowed to do that.

I'd asked Simon tentatively whether we should include Rod in plans for dinner as well as lunch, but he had been noncommittal. 'We'll just have to see how it goes'—which didn't help much with the catering. However, Rod refused my obligatory invitation, saying he had to be back at the hotel for a phone call he had booked.

'Then perhaps tomorrow?' I persisted, feeling I must know in advance to make adequate preparations.

'Thanks, that'd be swell.'

Simon drove him to the station and then joined me in the sitting room.

'There was no need to force the issue on a meal, you know. If we start a precedent it could be embarrassing.'

'There'd be no harm in making a regular thing of it. He'll only be here for another week, and from the letters I typed, I gather you'll be out for two full days visiting people.'

He didn't answer, and I went on, 'I thought we might ask Bill and Sally round tomorrow, instead of going to them. We owe them an invitation, anyway, and perhaps Jeremy and Sylvia could come too.'

'We don't want to get bogged down into a full-scale cocktail party.'

'It would hardly be that, but we needn't ask the Parkes if you don't want to. It just occurred to me that we haven't been very sociable since we came. The only people who've been to the house are Lucy and Sue, and that was when you were out.'

'All right, do as you think fit, but not more than those four, and make it clear when you invite them that it's for pre-dinner drinks only, otherwise they'll still be here at ten.'

Rod arrived the next morning looking pale and drawn. His wife, it appeared, had been taken into hospital as a precautionary measure.'

'I guess I won't be very good company this evening,' he said with an apologetic smile.

'It may help to take your mind off things. We've invited four friends round for drinks first—I think you'll like them. Bill Denver was in the States some years ago.'

'That's a good name he's got there, anyway,' Rod said with a ghost of his usual smile. 'Almost as good as mine!'

The day passed. I did a bit of typing, a bit of superficial filing to keep things tidy, and Simon and Rod pored over leaflets together and drew up lists of things they wanted to discuss at their appointments during the next two days.

At five I left them to put the final preparations in hand for dinner and to supervise the laying out of cocktail savouries. Then I had a leisurely bath, put on a new dress and went down to join them. Rod turned as I came in and gave a low, appreciative whistle.

'How does she do it?' he marvelled. 'At one moment the efficient, self-effacing secretary, the next the ravishing hostess! And boy, do I mean ravishing!'

I laughed. 'You'll make me blush if you go on like that, I'm not used to it!'

'Well if you're not, you surely ought to be. Any girl likes to be told when she looks good—and you always do.'

'Thank you, kind sir!' I said demurely, flashing a look at Simon beneath my lashes. But he had his back turned busy with the glasses, and gave no indication that he had heard the exchange. I glanced back at Rod and he closed one eye in a deliberate wink.

Rod and Bill found plenty to talk about, and he also seemed to strike an immediate rapport with Jeremy Parkes. They were much the same type, quiet and serious, with a kind of old-world charm.

'Your friends are delightful,' Rod said warmly when they dutifully left at eight o'clock. 'It was kind of you to invite them to meet me.'

'Well, you've seen enough of Simon and me. I thought you needed a change!' Slightly to my consternation, I was finding it was much easier to make light conversation with Rod than it was with Simon, and because I was aware of his continued worrying beneath the surface, I kept the flow going throughout dinner.

'So I won't see you again till Friday,' I remarked as he was leaving for the station with Simon. 'I do hope there'll have been some good news before that.'

He took my hand and squeezed it. 'Thanks, Cherry. And thanks for all you've done. It didn't escape my notice, the effort you made to keep me from brooding.' He hesitated for a moment, then bent forward and kissed my cheek. 'See you Friday.' He turned to Simon with a smile. 'Hope you don't mind, but she's been great.'

I stood at the door to watch them drive away, then I went up to bed. I hoped anxiously that Laurie would be all right. It would be too terrible if anything went wrong now.

Simon came straight up when he got back. 'You've certainly made a hit with our friend,' he remarked sourly.

'He's sweet, isn't he?'

'*Sweet*?' His lip curled in distaste.

'Well I think he is. And he's so obviously missing his wife and wishing he could be with her at this difficult time.'

'I don't know about *obviously* missing her. He pays enough attention to you, always remarking on your dress or your perfume, or something.'

'Perhaps,' I suggested wickedly, 'he thinks you don't appreciate me!'

He paused in the act of pulling off his tie. 'Do you think that?'

'Frequently!' I said lightly.

'Because I don't bombard you with chocolates and flowers and pretty speeches?'

'I'm not asking to be 'bombarded,' but the odd compliment wouldn't go amiss. After all, I do my best to please you.' I bit my lip, feeling like a charlady asking for a reference.

Simon said gruffly, 'If I were to remark on it every time you looked lovely it would be a trifle monotonous, because as Rod says you always do.'

I turned to him in surprise but he wasn't looking at me. 'Well,' I said a little breathlessly, 'that's worth quite a lot for a start.'

'I thought you knew my opinion.'

There was a lump in my throat. I went over to him, turned him to face me and slid my arms round his neck.

'Just tell me now and then,' I murmured. 'And for the record, I think you're lovely too!'

His hands caressed my bare shoulders. 'I'm not much of a husband for you, am I, Cherry? I realize that and it makes me surly and bad-tempered, but I can't seem to do anything about it.'

'I'm not complaining,' I said softly. It was on the tip of my tongue to ask him if he loved me, but it wouldn't have done any good. I didn't want an automatic, perhaps meaningless, reply. I wanted—needed—a voluntary declaration. And for the same reason, I couldn't say that I loved him lest he felt merely obliged to do the same. It was an impasse, and only when we had overcome it would the indefinable barriers dissolve once and for all. And that couldn't happen soon enough for me.

*   *   *

Sally phoned the next morning. 'Thanks for inviting us round, we did enjoy it. And you're

138

right, Rod is certainly dishy! Lucky you, with two attractive men under your feet all day!'

'They're not at the moment,' I told her. 'They're visiting clients today and tomorrow, so I've got a breather. Simon won't be home till late.'

'Actually, I rather gathered that last night, which is one reason why I'm phoning. I wonder if could ask you a favour?'

'Of course.'

'It's not actually for me, but for Bill's young sister. Today's her wedding anniversary—the first—and their baby sitter's let them down. She rang to see if I could help out, but I can't. We're going out ourselves this evening.'

I said dubiously, 'I've never done any babysitting. What does it involve?'

'Only giving her the ten o'clock feed, and it'll be left all ready for you. Apart from that, it's really only a question of watching their television instead of your own. Chris would call for you and run you home afterwards. Please, Cherry—it would mean such a lot to them.'

'All right, I'll do my best.'

Unenthusiastic even at the start, my anxiety increased as the day wore on, and I began to wonder in a panic what I should do if anything went wrong. By the time Chris called for me as arranged, I was almost ready to take back my offer, but he didn't give me the chance.

'It is kind of you to step into the breach like

139

this. Angie was almost in tears this morning, when Mrs. Barker let us down. We haven't been out since the baby was born and she was so looking forward to it.'

'As long as she's prepared to trust me with it,' I said dubiously.

He laughed. 'You can't go wrong. Charlotte's a gem. We've never had a disturbed night with her yet.'

'How old is she?'

'Six weeks.'

Six weeks! I should be terrified of breaking her!

Angie was waiting anxiously in the hall—a tall, pretty girl with a mane of long hair. She didn't look old enough to be anyone's mother—but Cathy had been much the same age when James was born.

'How good of you to come, Mrs. Slade. If you'd like to come upstairs, I'll show you where everything is.'

The nursery was warm, and in shadow. A baby trolley stood against one wall, with a mattress on top and a pile of nappies on a shelf beneath.

'There's no point in changing her before the feed, she'd only be wet again when you'd finished. The nappy pail's here, and the baby powder.'

'I've never changed a nappy,' I confessed miserably. That was something Sally had omitted to mention.

'It's quite easy. Fold it like this: there, I'll leave this one ready for you. And put your finger under the pin as you fasten it, so it can't prick her. Her feed's in this warmer. It just needs plugging in ten minutes beforehand. Shake a few drops on the back of your hand to make sure it's the right temperature—blood heat—and stop every now and then to rub her back. Okay?'

'I think so.' I glanced apprehensively in the direction of the cot. 'May I peep?'

'Of course. She's just finished her six o'clock feed, so she's dead to the world!' She bent over the cot, her hair falling forward like a curtain. I joined her, unprepared for the smallness of the dark head lying there.

'I didn't realize she'd be quite so tiny!' I stammered.

Angie took this as a mild insult. 'She's not *small*! She put on four ounces in the last week. She weighs nine pounds now.'

'I mean so—helpless,' I amended apologetically. Her mother smiled, a particularly sweet, tender smile.

'Yes, I know. It almost makes me cry some times, to think how defenceless she is.'

Her husband appeared in the doorway. 'I don't want to rush you, darling, but if Mrs. Slade's happy I think we should go.'

'Yes. of course. The sitting room's on the left downstairs and I've left a tray for you in the kitchen. Do make yourself some coffee

141

when you want it. We'll be back between eleven and half past, if that's all right?'

'Yes, fine.' I couldn't tear my eyes away from that tiny, sleeping face.

Angie said, 'Don't worry about her. You'll need to wake her when you're ready—she sleeps like a top. See you later then.'

She hesitated, and when I made no move to join her, left me and went downstairs to Chris. A minute later I heard the front door close quietly. I was alone with the baby.

I bent over the cot again, and a sweet, unfamiliar smell rose to meet me, compounded of damp blanket and talcum powder. One tiny hand was curled under her cheek. I had never seen so small a baby before. In fact, the only baby I had remotely come in contact with had been Anna on that brief visit six years ago, and she had then been about three months.

I continued my inspection with absorbed interest. The little face was cream-coloured, the dark hair soft as swan's-down. A thick fringe of lashes lay like a curtain on the round cheek. For the very first time I felt a peculiar ache, a kind of yearning, and I silently cursed Sally for exposing me to this propaganda—and I had no doubt that was what it was. I stayed a few minutes more. Once she made little snuffling noises like a small animal, smacking her lips. I half hoped she'd open her eyes so that I could have the excuse of picking her up. But she showed no signs of waking and eventually I went softly downstairs and into the pleasant sitting room. The television had been left on low, and there was a pile of magazines on a table.

I sat down and tried to concentrate on the programme, but half my mind was upstairs in the nursery. During a commercial break, I ran back upstairs and hung over the crib. The baby hadn't moved. Back I went to the meaningless television. After a few minutes I gave up, switched it off, and flicked through the magazines. At a quarter to ten, I reminded myself, the bottle warmer must be plugged in. It was now seven-thirty.

I went into the kitchen and made myself some coffee, not because I was thirsty but for something to do. There was a covered bowl with a feeding bottle and teats in it, and nappies hung on the rack. The fridge, when I took out the milk, was full of jars of baby food. The house was entirely baby-oriented.

I carried the coffee back to my chair and looked through some more magazines. *Planning Baby's Layette*, *Baby's First Year*. I was not to be allowed to forget my charge. At last, since I couldn't settle downstairs, I took a few magazines with me and made my way back to the nursery. I pushed the low basket nursing chair over to the cot and sat down. I couldn't see Charlotte's face because she was facing the wall, but I could see the soft dark hair through the rails and an incredibly vulnerable-looking

143

little indentation in the nape of her neck. I leaned back in my chair, trying not to analyze the restlessness I'd felt downstairs and the peace which filled me now, but I couldn't suppress the thought: suppose this baby was mine and Simon's? My heart gave a little jerk, instantly stilled. I must at all costs keep myself free to be with Simon.

I sat quietly beside the Cot for almost two hours, sometimes glancing at a magazine, sometimes letting my thoughts go where they would. And at the allotted time, I went downstairs to prepare the bottle.

The baby was still sound asleep. Did she know her name? My mind fluttered uselessly over the training of puppies.

'Charlotte,' I said softly, 'supper time!'

I slid my arm carefully under the little body, and all my apprehension vanished in a wave of eagerness. At last the eyes opened and gazed up at me, dark and unfathomable. I picked her up and held her against me. Immediately the little head turned, the open mouth searching at my breast. My eyes filled with hot tears. I lowered myself carefully into the chair and reached for the bottle.

The next half hour was full of wonder. Charlotte sucked strongly, one minute hand resting contentedly on the bottle. Patting her back, I felt a thrill of achievement when the wind duly came up. Even the nappy change proceeded without a hitch, and by that time her eyes were already closing again.

I wrapped her in the shawl and stood rocking her gently, reluctant to put her down. The little head, top-heavy on the slender stem of neck, lolled contentedly against my shoulder. At last, with a sigh I didn't define, I laid her back in the cot and drew the covers over her. My services were at an end. I picked up the empty bottle and took it down to the kitchen, where I rinsed it along with my coffee cup. I was drying the saucer when Angie and Chris returned. Angie appeared at the kitchen door.

'Oh, don't bother with that, please. How did you get on?'

'Marvellously. She's absolutely gorgeous, isn't she?' Then, more usefully, I added, 'She had the whole bottle and got her wind up with no bother. And I handled the nappy business like a pro!'

She laughed. 'I realize it was a bit of an ordeal for you. Sally said you weren't used to babies. It was sweet of you to come. Here's a little something for helping us out.'

She handed me a box of chocolates and brushed aside my thanks. 'Chris will run you home. I hope your husband won't mind your being rather late.'

Simon, surprisingly, was in bed when I arrived home.

'What's this about baby-sitting? You, of all people!'

'It was Bill's sister's baby. The woman they usually have let them down and it was their wedding anniversary. Oh Simon, she was gorgeous!'

'Bill's sister, or the woman who let her down?'

'Stupid! She was so tiny and so perfect!'

He was looking at me with a little smile.

'Don't think I've changed my mind, though.' My voice was sharper than I'd intended and his smile disappeared. 'Anyway, you've got three,' I added lightly. 'You mustn't be greedy!' But he hadn't got them—Cathy had.

*   *   *

Simon was out again all the next day, and late coming home in the evening. I went shopping. I did some gardening. And I tried to stop thinking of baby Charlotte. Our marriage was rocky enough now, when it was receiving my full attention. Although I hated myself for it, there was no denying that I was a little jealous of Simon's children and their share of his love, which they took so much for granted. To be jealous of my own baby would be intolerable. It was ludicrous, I told myself fiercely, that all my carefully worked out reasoning should be knocked sideways by a few hours' contact with someone else's baby.

'Any news of Rod's wife?' I asked Simon that evening.

146

'No change, I gather. Most unfortunate it should be while he's so far away. If what he's doing now wasn't the culmination of about two years' planning, he'd be home like a shot.'

The next morning, dark smudges under his eyes told of Rod's restless night. His anxiety was now a tangible thing, an extra presence with us in the office.

Just before midday, Simon pushed back his chair. 'I think I'll take these letters along to the Post Office to be sure of catching the noon collection.'

While he was gone the telephone rang and I picked it up.

'Cheston 254?'

The line crackled in my ear. 'This is Chicago, Illinois. I have a person-to-person call for Mr. Rod Cleveland. Is he with you, please? The Carlton Hotel gave me your number.'

I felt myself go very hot. 'Yes, yes he is. One moment. Rod, it's for you. Chicago.'

He stared at me for a moment, then he was across the room in a leap and had taken the receiver from my hand. 'Yes—yes. Who's calling?'

Quietly, I let myself out of the room and closed the door. I went into the bedroom and stood for a moment gazing at my reflection in the full-length mirror. Let it be all right! Let it be all right!

I turned away and went downstairs. The

dining room table was laid ready for lunch and, in the kitchen, Mrs. Charles, in complete charge today, had the meal well under way. The phone in the hall gave a little ring, indicating that the extension had been replaced. Fearfully, I went back upstairs.

I knew as soon as I opened the door. Rod was standing in the middle of the room, his face chalky, and a dazed expression in his eyes. He said flatly, 'She's lost the baby. She's going to be all right, but she's lost the baby.' His voice cracked.

I said sharply, 'Oh, no!' A picture of little Charlotte flashed across my mind. 'Oh Rod, no!'

I don't know which of us moved, but I had him tight in my arms, holding his shuddering body against mine and trying to instill some grain of comfort. And that was how Simon found us. He stood for one moment in the doorway and then the door closed behind him. Rod moved blunderingly away.

'It's all right,' I said, 'he understands.' Whether this was true or not, I did not at that moment care. I went on quickly, 'The main thing is that Laurie's all right.'

'All right physically,' he corrected heavily. 'I don't know what this will do to her. Oh God, I ought to be *there*!' He pounded one hand into the palm of the other.

'There'll be other babies.'

He gave a despairing little shrug. 'It took us

five years to start this one. And we wanted it so much.'

I moistened my lips. 'Was it Laurie on the phone?'

'No, she's not come round yet. They had to give her an anesthetic. It was her mother who called. She's been at the hospital all night. It's about six in the morning over there.'

'Well, it's what you've been dreading, and now that it's happened at least you needn't fear it anymore. Let's go and find Simon and get a good strong drink inside us.'

Simon had already poured the drinks. He didn't look up as we went into the room. I said shakily. 'There was a call from Chicago. Laurie's all right, but she's lost the baby.'

'I'm sorry.' He didn't look at either of us and there was a muscle jumping in his cheek. He handed us each a glass and Rod drank his at a gulp.

'Thanks. I needed that.'

'Would you like to go back to town after lunch?'

'Not immediately, but this means I'll have to go home, Simon. I'm sorry as hell to be letting you down like this, but I have no option.'

'Of course. I understand that. We've covered most things at this end anyway.'

'Yeah. Perhaps we can finalize the details of the Jonson contract this afternoon, then at least that'll be clear. I'll book the first flight available when I get back to the hotel.'

So at four o'clock Rod came down with Simon for the last time. He took my hand in his. 'I hate goodbyes, especially under these conditions. You and Simon must come over to the States sometime and let me repay some of your hospitality. In the meantime, I have to get back as quick as I can and try to convince Laurie that the world hasn't come to an end, as you did with me. Bless you for it, and for being there when I badly needed someone.'

I lifted my face to receive his kiss. 'Give her my love,' I said.

I waited, with some trepidation, for Simon's return from the station. I knew we were in for disturbances of some sort and I felt too drained to cope with them. I sat back in the easy chair and closed my eyes, not opening them when he came back into the room.

He said levelly, 'That was a tender little scene I came in on up there.'

I kept my eyes shut. 'He was desperately in need of comfort.'

His voice shook. 'Did you have to hold him like that?'

'It was all I could think of. No, I didn't even think. It was pure instinct, like going to help a child that was hurt.'

'Except that Rod is not a child. It's been obvious all along that he regarded you as some kind of wife substitute. He said you even looked like her. All week we've had smiles and compliments, and I've had to watch you flirting—'

'I was *not* flirting!' I cried furiously.

'I don't know what else you'd call it. And you never stopped singing his praises: 'Rod is so polite, Rod is so *sweet*!' His voice was venomous. 'And finally, today. How do you think I felt when I came in on you like that? I didn't know about the phone call, remember. It just looked as though as soon as I was out of the way—'

He broke off, trying to control his breathing, but I was powerless to take advantage of the pause to defend myself.

'Anyway,' he continued after a moment. 'I can't say I'm sorry he's gone. If I'd known the way things would be, I'd never have brought him back here, office or no office.'

I rose to my feet and began to make my way blindly to the door.

'Where are you going? I haven't finished speaking to you! Cathy!'

I stopped dead. *'Don't call me Cathy!'*

He said quickly. 'I'm sorry, that was just a slip of the tongue. You know that. I only—'

But I'd had enough. I ran from the room up the stairs and flung myself down on the bed, all the tension and strain of the last months releasing themselves in a torrent of weeping. It was some time later that Simon came upstairs.

'Now, that will do,' he said quietly. 'Sit up and I'll sponge your face.'

I pushed myself into a sitting position, and

he dabbed gently at my swollen eyes with an ice-cold towel he had brought from the bathroom. His face was white but his eyes weren't hard any more.

'There, that's better. Now come downstairs like a good girl and have some dinner.'

'No, I—'

'Yes. You hardly ate any lunch—none of us did.' He looked down at the towel in his hands. 'Cherry, I said some pretty rotten things. The plain truth is that I was jealous. You don't laugh and chatter to me as you did with Rod, but no doubt that's my fault rather than yours. And, of course, it was unforgivable to call you Cathy. So once again I find myself having to apologize to you. I'm afraid it's becoming a regular occurrence.'

'You've no need to feel jealous, Simon,' I said wearily. 'Ever.' But I couldn't summon up any comfort in the admission because, once again, I didn't believe it. It was a convenient excuse for his loss of temper. He hadn't thought I cared enough to be jealous of his association with Rona. Now the positions were reversed.

'Am I forgiven?'

'Yes. of course.'

'Come along, then. You'll feel better when you've had something to eat.'

And with his arm round my shoulders, we went down to dinner.

CHAPTER NINE

The summer dragged on. Simon continued to work at home and I did odd bits of typing and filing for him. Since the storm over Rod, he went out of his way to be considerate and gentle with me, but underneath there was still an appalling sense of strain.

It was, of course, the long school holidays. Sally and Bill were away for three weeks, but even when they returned she was too involved with the children to provide the company I craved. I considered going up to London to visit Sue and Lucy, but I was bedevilled by an insidious listlessness which I couldn't shake off. It was easier to lie on a rug in the garden, reading and sleeping through the long, hot days.

'You need a holiday,' Simon said one day, a little crease of concern between his eyes. 'We both do, for that matter. I really should have booked before this. Where would you like to go?'

'I leave it to you,' I said without interest. I left everything to him nowadays.

'A holiday will buck you up,' he said rallyingly. 'It hasn't been an easy summer.'

But it was not over yet, and another trial awaited us.

I wasn't sleeping very well, so it was I who

heard the phone first, clanging away in the darkness like an alarm bell. I jumped out of bed, my heart pounding as I felt for the light switch. Five o'clock! Who could be phoning at such an hour? As I sped out of the door, I heard Simon sit up.

'What is it? What's happening?'

I didn't stop to reply. The shaft of light from the open door lit the landing sufficiently for me to make my way to the extension phone in the office. The curtains in there were not drawn and the room was filled with the eerie light of dawn.

'Yes? Cheston 254?'

Fantastically, like some projection of a nightmare, it was Cathy's voice, raw with nerves.

'Is Simon there, Cherry? I must speak to him!'

I handed him the receiver as he hurried barefoot into the room.

'Cathy,' I said simply, and stood shivering in my nightdress, trying to fight down a growing sense of panic.

'Cathy! What—? When did this happen? Why wasn't I told?'

Her voice echoed through the mouthpiece but I couldn't distinguish the words. My eyes strained through the unreal light to read his tense face.

'They've just taken him in now? Right, I'll be with you in—' he automatically glanced at his wrist, realized that of course he wasn't wearing his watch. 'Well, just as soon as I can. I'll pack a case and leave straight away. Try not to worry.'

He put down the phone and stood for a moment, leaning his weight on it. I was encased in ice.

'Simon, what is it?'

Slowly he straightened and turned to me. 'It's James. He's been rushed off to hospital with appendicitis. They think it might have burst.'

I stared at him, while my mind flicked slowly through an assortment of pictures like a broken film projector. James complaining of tummyache, being sick—and Simon writing it off as an attempt to gain attention. I longed to comfort him, but I hadn't gone to him instinctively as I had to Rod in this same horrible room, and by the time I registered that I should have done, it was too late. I made a movement but he seemed to come back to earth and walked quickly past me back to the bedroom, unbuttoning his pyjama jacket as he went.

'Will you make me a flask of coffee and a few sandwiches? I'll just fling some things into a case. Where are the cases, for God's sake?'

'Up there.' I pointed to the top of his wardrobe. The import of his words slowly sank in. 'I'm coming with you, you know.'

He paused fractionally. 'There's no point.

I'll have to be with Cathy—it might be difficult for you.'

'I tell you I'm coming!' My voice rose.

'All right, I haven't time to argue. But hurry—coffee and sandwiches, and just your nightdress and toothbrush.'

Quickly and clumsily, my hands clammy, I dressed, folded my still warm nightdress and laid it on top of Simon's clothes in the case.

There was a cold joint of meat in the fridge. I hacked slices off it and put them between buttered bread. Please let him be all right— please let him be all right.

Simon appeared in the doorway as I poured scalding coffee into the flask. 'I've told Mrs. Charles. Are you sure you wouldn't rather stay here?'

'Quite sure.' I looked at his grey face fearfully. 'Oh darling, it'll be all right. You'll see, by the time we get there the worst will be over.'

But my comfort couldn't reach him; it had been offered too late. I had failed him when he most needed me, where I had not failed Rod who meant less to me than Simon's little finger. I ached with an intolerable burden of guilt. The point was, of course, that with Rod I'd been half-expecting the news and my sympathy had been completely for him. The impact of the shock about James was on a much deeper, more personal level, involving myself as much as Simon, and my first reaction

156

had been to remember the warning signs we'd ignored. By the time I'd pushed through them to think of Simon, the harm was done and there was no way to explain my lapse. Any attempt to do so would only emphasize it.

We were away before five-thirty, driving through the greyness of a day that had not yet dawned, a day which, if all did not go right, might remain grey with us forever. We had left Mrs. Charles in the hall, her hair in braids, clutching her faded blue dressing gown.

'You will phone and let me know, sir? You'll tell me how he goes on?'

'Just as soon as we have any definite news,' Simon had promised, and laid a hand gently on her arm. No doubt it seemed to him that she was more upset than I was. After all, she'd known the child from birth. I thought of James's pathetic lapse to babyhood in his moment of pain: 'I want my mummy!' No doubt, knowing Cathy, she was with him now.

'Did she phone from the hospital?' I asked, breaking a long silence.

'Yes. She'd waited till they took him to the operating theatre. Poor little devil—it must have been frightening for him.'

I didn't refer to the previous bout of sickness, but there was no need. I was aware that Simon's sense of guilt exceeded mine. As though reading my mind, he said in a low voice, 'And I thought it was all an act!'

'You couldn't have known,' I whispered.

'But I should have made sure. If I hadn't been so annoyed with him, I would have done. As it was, I left it all to you and didn't even go near him. If anything—'

'Stop it!' I said sharply.

'I didn't even arrange for them to come down during August. I thought it would have been too much for you in the circumstances, but he probably just thought I hadn't forgiven him.'

So it was my fault too. Well, if it helped him to apportion the blame, I was more than willing to accept it.

We turned onto the motorway, merging with the great lorries that had been travelling through the night. Some of the cars, their roofs piled with luggage, obviously belonged to families making an early start on their holidays. Simon's foot went down on the accelerator. Trees and hedges shot past us with dismaying speed, and still this inner coldness spread through my body.

'Tell me when you'd like some coffee.'

'Let's get some mileage under our wheels before we stop, but if you can extract a sandwich, that would be welcome. I'm feeling somewhat empty.'

I knew what he meant. In silence, we bit into the succulent meat. I remembered Simon carving it on Sunday, with the sun streaming through the dining room windows. How relatively happy we'd been then, compared with this gnawing fear.

I began to long for the warmth and stimulation of the coffee. Simon's hand when he took the sandwich had been as cold as mine. After that first moment in the office, the moment I'd wasted, he had shut himself up with his unbearable worry, tacitly assuming that it didn't touch me nearly as deeply. There was no way to get close to him. Perhaps there never had been.

If the silence was ever to be broken, it seemed it must always be by me.

'When did it start? Did she say?'

'Apparently he was off-colour yesterday, first just stomach pains then at lunch time he started vomiting. After that he slept for a while, and she thought he was over it. But it started again, much worse, about two o'clock this morning. She panicked—thank God she did—and phoned the doctor. He had the ambulance there almost immediately.'

I glanced at his set jaw, the hardness in his eyes. 'Darling, do you think we could stop at the next service station? I could use some coffee now.'

Five minutes he allowed us, no more. We didn't even get out of the car, but sat with our hands clasped around the plastic cups and sipped at the wonderful hot liquid. We finished the sandwiches and then were off again, back into the now steady stream of traffic moving north.

'It's still a bit early to phone,' Simon said. 'We'll stop again in about half an hour.'

I was stiff and cramped from sitting so long in one position. It was five and a half months since we had last come along this road, to confront my parents with our wedding plans. I wondered if we would ever travel it happily.

We left the motorway just after ten o'clock. I had to look twice at my watch: it felt like tea time. A couple of hours had now passed since Simon's telephone call, and the formal hospital phrase had done little to ease our anxiety. 'He's now back in the ward but still under the anaesthetic.'

We had decided to go Aunt Beth's house rather than the hospital. Simon had said something about visiting hours, but I suspected that he was half-afraid of what he might find there. We'd left a message for Cathy that we'd be at her mother's just after ten-thirty. I wondered briefly if my parents knew of our headlong flight. I hadn't had time to contact them, but Simon and I would need a bed. We could hardly sleep at Cathy's.

At last we reached the turning into Aunt Beth's road, and the car drew up outside the house. For a moment, Simon sat with his hands gripping the wheel, his head slightly bowed. Then he opened the door and came round to my side. It was as I stepped out of the car that the front door burst open and Cathy came flying down the path.

'Simon! Oh Simon, thank God you've come!' Without pause for thought she flung herself into his arms. Above her tousled hair his face was unreadable.

He said with difficulty, 'There's—no further news?'

'No, none.' She seemed to recollect herself slightly. 'I'm sorry, I shouldn't have done that.'

Simon said brusquely, 'Forget it. All that matters now is James.'

'Yes.' She wiped the back of her hand across her face, leaving a dirty streak which made her appear young and vulnerable. 'We can go along at two. He should be fully conscious then. He was very dopey when I left him, rambling and not knowing what he was saying. It was terrifying, even though I knew it was only the anaesthetic.'

'Had the appendix burst?'

A tremor fluttered her mouth. 'I'm afraid so. There's a tube in, and you'd better brace yourself for an intravenous as well. He became dehydrated, with being sick so much.'

'Cathy, I've got to tell you this. He had an attack when he was with us. I did nothing about it. I'll never forgive myself.'

'Oh Simon, don't!' Her face twisted and she gripped his hand with both hers. They seemed entirely oblivious of me. 'Don't blame yourself. He was always having stomach upsets—lots of children do. There was no way you could have known.'

I said—and my voice cracked—'Take Cathy in, Simon. We should phone Mother as soon as possible.'

We made our way up the path. Aunt Beth was in the hall. I wondered how she would greet me, but it was no time for recriminations. I had Cathy's husband, but at least I'd brought him back when she needed him. She put up her cheek for his kiss as she must so often have done in the past.

'Your parents are expecting you, Cherry. I'm afraid we haven't room to put you up here.'

'No, of course not. I was just going to phone them.'

She said automatically, 'You must be tired after the long journey. Come through—I've some coffee ready.'

The house had recently been converted into two flats, and now Aunt Beth lived upstairs and Cathy and the children below. We went into the front room and found Paul and Anna, unusually subdued, their faces pale and frightened. Simon held out his arms and they both ran to him. I glanced at Cathy and caught a strange expression on her face. Surely it couldn't be jealousy?

We sat around drinking coffee, trying not to catch each other's eyes. Aunt Beth said. 'I thought we'd have a light lunch here, Simon, then you and Cathy can drop Cherry off at Ellen's on your way to the hospital.'

No one made any comment. The child was

only allowed two visitors and obviously they must be his parents. So I shouldn't have the chance to be with Simon when he looked at his son in that pitiful condition. Cathy would have to support him, and he her. After all, James was their child. I had no claim on him.

Simon said, 'Wouldn't it be a good idea if Cathy had a rest before lunch? She must be exhausted.'

'Yes,' my aunt agreed. 'I tried to get her to nap earlier, but she wouldn't until you arrived.'

'Well, I'm here now, Cathy, you can relax a little.'

Her taut face softened in a little smile. She nodded, and went quietly out of the room.

'Will you read us a story, Daddy?' Paul suggested hopefully.

'No, Paul, don't bother your father now.'

'It's all right, I'll read to them. It will pass the time.' I knew he was incapable just then of denying the children anything, lest more retribution should follow.

Paul brought a story book, and Anna perched on Simon's knee. I leaned back and closed my eyes. If only I could wake from this horrible dream and find myself at the beginning of a blessedly normal day at home, with Simon working in the office upstairs and Mrs. Charles's John on his knees by the rose bed. I wished the children would leave us. If I only had Simon to myself at that moment, nothing would stop me telling him how much he meant to me. In my mind's eye, I saw him standing at the gate with Cathy clutched in his arms. Perhaps this crisis, however it ended, would show them that they couldn't live without each other after all.

I stood up suddenly, and the other three looked up. 'I'm going into the garden,' I said jerkily. I didn't want to face Aunt Beth in the kitchen so I went out of the front door and round the side of the house. The old swing where Cathy and I had played as children was still there. I wandered about aimlessly, running my fingers over the velvety petals of the flowers. Finally, in a primeval need for the comfort of rocking, I sat on the swing and drifted to and fro. After a while Cathy came to join me.

'I saw you from the bedroom window. I couldn't settle after all. You must be tired too, Cherry.'

'Yes.'

She hesitated: 'Look, I'm sorry about that business when you arrived. It was simply overwhelming relief at not being alone any more.'

'It's all right, I understood.'

She looked at me oddly. 'I don't think you did really. Not having children of your own, you couldn't possibly. You see, despite everything that's happened, Simon's the only one who can help me through this. No one else, not even Mother. But you must understand that I only regard him as James's father—my child's father. Nothing else.'

I said quietly, 'You didn't have to explain, but thank you.' No one would tell me in which light Simon was thinking of her.

'You've not changed your mind about marrying again?' I'd feel so much safer if she did.

'Bruce? No, he knows there's no chance of that. We enjoy going around together, but that's all.'

'Lunch is ready!' Aunt Beth called from the back door. I almost expected her to add, as she had done so often, 'And wipe your feet *carefully* as you come in!'

Cathy said quickly, 'Please, Cherry, don't grudge me Simon just now. I'm nearly going out of my mind.'

'I know. Forget about me.'

But would Simon tamely submit to being handed back to me when Cathy's need of him had passed?

It was a silent meal and even the children scarcely touched their food. As soon as it was over we went out to the car.

'I'll sit in the back,' I said brightly, 'since you're dropping me first.' Neither of them made any comment. When we stopped at my parents' gate, I picked up the case with our night clothes and got out quickly.

'You will phone, won't you? To let me know how he is and when to expect you?'

'Yes, of course.'

I stood at the gate watching them drive away until Cathy's fair head and Simon's dark one seemed to swim together in a haze of tears.

'Hello, love.' I turned to find my father beside me. Wordlessly, I buried my face in his jacket and he held me tightly. 'There, there, little one. You've had a bad time, I know. Give me the case and come inside.'

'Cherry, darling!' It was the first spontaneous greeting I'd had from my mother since my engagement. 'You look absolutely washed out!'

'So would you,' I said with a touch of grim humour, 'if you'd been up since five o'clock!'

'Yes, of course. But you've lost weight too, haven't you? Your face is certainly thinner.'

I turned away from her scrutiny. 'I'm all right, Mum.'

'How's Cathy?'

'Distraught.' There was no other description.

'Poor child.' I wasn't sure if she meant Cathy or James. 'Would you like to go upstairs for a while, dear, and rest? We'll wake you if there's any news.'

'I think I would, please.' I had an urgent need to be alone for a while, to rebuild my defences.

'I'll bring the case up,' Father said. Automatically, I turned into my old room.

Then my eyes fell on the narrow bed and I stopped. Father said apologetically, 'We've had to put Simon in the guest room again, I'm afraid, and there isn't a double bed in there, either.'

'It doesn't matter.'

But it did. I knew that tonight of all nights I should need the comfort of his arms. Father put the case on the floor and drew the curtains to shut out the afternoon sunshine. He kissed me gently.

'Try to sleep, love, it'll do you good.'

The door closed softly behind him. I slipped out of the creased dress I had fumbled into so many hours ago, realizing with dismay that it was the only one I had with me. Then I crept under the covers and lay looking at the familiar layout of the room that had been mine for as long as I could remember. When I closed my eyes, it seemed that I was still in the car beside Simon, with the rushing trees and fields. But Simon was with Cathy now. Forget it. Forget everything. Suddenly, with no preliminaries, I was asleep.

*   *   *

It was four o'clock when I awoke, and the shadows had lengthened on the ceiling. I padded out onto the landing and leaned over the bannisters.

'Mum?'

My mother came out into the hall. 'Did you have a good sleep?'

'Wonderful, thank you. Has there been any news?'

'No, nothing. They're probably still with him.'

'Will it be all right if I have a bath?'

'Of course. And tea will be ready when you come down.'

The warm water completed the good work done by my sleep. I felt much better. I brushed my hair carefully and put on some make-up for the first time that day. I had just reached the hall when the phone rang. I snatched it up.

'Hello, dear. Sorry to be late phoning but we weren't allowed in to see him till four. He was asleep and obviously they didn't want to wake him. We couldn't stay long, but they say we can go back at seven. Cathy suggests I have supper with them rather than hold you up, and I'll be with you about ten. Is that all right?'

Five hours till I could see him. 'Yes, that seems sensible. How is he?'

'Not too good, I'm afraid. I'm hoping he looks worse than he is, with all those ghastly tubes and things. They say quite a lot of the fluid seems to be seeping away, which is a good thing, of course. I might know more when I see you later. How are you feeling?'

'I've had a sleep and a bath, and feel much better. I wish you could do the same.'

'That'll have to wait, I'm afraid. We're just

168

going for a cup of tea now. See you later, then.'

I went slowly through to the sitting room to join my parents for tea.

Somehow the hours crawled past. At one stage I asked, as the thought struck me for the first time, 'Shouldn't you be at work, Dad?'

'It's the last week of his holiday,' Mother explained. 'Has Simon made any arrangements about being away from work?'

'Not as far as I know but he's working at home at the moment anyway because they're in the process of moving offices. We ought to let someone know, though.' Perhaps I, in my secretarial capacity, should have thought of that earlier, though if they phoned through to the house no doubt Mrs. Charles would explain.

The television was switched on. A play—incomprehensible words. When would he come? The news came on at ten. And right on cue, my ears caught the sound of the car at the gate. I almost ran out, but memories were too recent of Cathy doing exactly that. I went into the hall and waited at the front door. He came in, pushed it closed behind him, and came straight into my arms. For what seemed a long time, we stood absolutely still, hanging onto each other. Then he gave a little sigh and kissed me.

'I needed that.'

'Me too.'

'Cherry my sweet, what a hell of a day!'

'Yes . . . any change?'

'Not as far as I can tell.'

'How's Cathy?'

'Much the same, too. I managed to calm her down a bit, I think. What frightens her is that she can't find anyone who will look her straight in the eye and say categorically that he's going to be all right.'

'But he is, isn't he?'

He gave a short laugh. 'My dear love, if a doctor won't commit himself, how can I?'

I said carefully, because I had to know, 'Then he's not out of danger yet?'

'I'm afraid not. He won't be until they get rid of all the poison.'

I said, entirely without relevance, 'I'm afraid you're in the guest room. There isn't a double bed.'

'That's all I need!'

'And shouldn't you phone the office tomorrow?' I was saying everything that had to be said at once—in case, in this suddenly uncertain world, he was snatched away from me again.

'Yes, tomorrow. Now we'd better go in to the parents and make polite noises.'

'They've been very sweet, Simon.'

'So they should be, to you. I doubt if they'll be sweet to me.'

Actually, they were. Perhaps his haggard face wrung their hearts as it did mine. Father poured him a stiff whisky and as soon as he'd finished it, said briskly, 'You two go on up, don't wait for us. Simon looks dead on his feet.'

We were only too glad to go. On the landing Simon kissed me good night. 'Sleep well, sweetheart. Tomorrow's another day, thank God.'

I washed and undressed and crept into bed. I heard my parents come up and move around. Then the landing light clicked off and their door closed. My body was trembling in what I could only suppose was an excess of fatigue. Whatever accounted for it I couldn't stop, and it wouldn't let me sleep. After a while I was aware of a faint click. I stiffened, hardly daring to hope. The next moment my door opened soundlessly. Simon walked softly over to the bed and stood looking down at me.

'I'm not asleep,' I whispered.

'Good. It was awfully lonely in there. I didn't think you'd still be awake, but I just wanted to look at you. To make sure you were really here.'

'Oh, darling!'

'There's not much room, is there? Never mind, I just want to hold you for a little while.'

He slid in beside me, his breath warm on my face. I moved my lips softly along the groove of his cheek. After a while his breathing deepened and he slept.

I lay motionless for some time, holding him.

There was not enough room for two to sleep comfortably, but I couldn't wake him when he needed sleep so much. Inch by inch I slid out of the warm bed, kissed him gently and made my way shiveringly to the deserted guest room. His watch was on the bedside table, as it always was at home. Somehow there was comfort in this—and also in the fact that, despite all those hours with Cathy, he had still needed me. With a little sigh I lay down, pulled the pillow into my neck, and at last fell asleep.

CHAPTER TEN

If my mother was surprised to find Simon and me in each other's rooms the next morning, she made no comment and I volunteered none. While I was helping her cook breakfast, he made his phone calls: first to the hospital, second to the office, third to Cathy. He reported the results as we ate. The office wasn't worried by his absence. It was holiday time anyway and the reins were slackened. At the hospital there was no news. James had had a reasonably restful night but his temperature was still causing anxiety. He could see his parents at ten o'clock.

I said tentatively, 'If you're going again this afternoon, do you think I could see him? Just for a few minutes—I don't want to poach on Cathy's time.'

'I'm sure it will be all right. He's only allowed two visitors at a time, but I could wait outside while you go in with Cathy.'

I opened my mouth to suggest an alternative and closed it again. It was enough that my request should be considered.

'In that case, bring Cathy back here for lunch,' Mother suggested.

At lunch time the news was not so good. Cathy was convinced James seemed less well than the day before. 'He's more listless and his eyes aren't so bright,' she kept saying.

'Would you rather I didn't go?'

'Of course not, Cherry. A new face might cheer him up.'

I doubted that mine would but I genuinely wanted to see him. I had my own share of Simon's guilt. I had been the cause of the rift.

Despite their warnings, I felt a clutch of terror when I stood looking down at the bed. The monstrous intravenous, like some space age machine, towered over him, the needle disappearing into the bandage on the thin, childish arm. What struck me overwhelmingly was how small he looked, even in the narrow hospital bed, so pathetically small. I forced my mouth into a smile.

'Hello, James. What on earth have you been up to?'

He smiled a little. 'It must have been this all

the time.'

Simon was beside me. Cathy had insisted on waiting outside during my visit. 'Cherry's brought you some presents.'

Awkwardly I laid them on the bedside table—conventional grapes which I wasn't sure he was allowed, a pile of assorted comics.

'Thanks.' It seemed an effort for him to speak. The face propped up against the mound of pillows was as white as they were, and his hand when I took it felt dry and feverish.

'I'm thirsty,' he said fretfully. 'They'll only let me have tiny sips. And I'm sick of this intravenous—it hurts and I can't move about properly.'

'You mustn't move too much anyway or the wound won't heal.'

'It won't heal in any case until they take the tube out,' remarked James with logic. 'Dad, will you ask them when they'll take the intravenous away?'

'Yes. James, I'll try to find out for you.' Simon's eyes were dark with concern.

'Hasn't Mum come?'

'Oh yes,' I assured him hastily. 'She's lending me a little of her time because I wanted to see you. Shall I get her now?'

'It doesn't matter,' he said listlessly.

'Perhaps I'd better be going anyway. I'll come and see you again soon. Hurry up and get well, James. We all miss you.' I bent down and kissed the small hot face. To my surprise he reached out a hand and caught mine.

'Thanks for coming to see me,' he said, and the intentness of his eyes on mine willed me to understand that he was offering a truce.

'Just get better,' I said unsteadily, 'then we can all start again, can't we?'

He nodded, satisfied that I had got the message.

Simon said, 'I'll send Mummy In. I'll take Cherry home and be right back.'

'I can get a bus.'

'Don't be ridiculous.'

We found Cathy in the waiting room. 'How did he seem?'

'The same as this morning.'

As we came out onto the broad steps of the hospital I almost wished that I hadn't seen James. Like Simon, I could only hope he was not as bad as he looked. In the circumstances, his offer of friendship was especially poignant. It wasn't until Simon took my arm and squeezed it that I realized I was crying.

'I'm sorry—this isn't helping you. It's just—well, he didn't look too good, did he?'

'The understatement of the week!'

'But if the poison's coming away—' Something in his face stopped me. 'What is it?'

'Don't say anything to Cathy for the moment, but it seems to have stopped oozing.'

'But—isn't that good?'

'No, because they know from his

temperature that there's still poison there somewhere. And if it's not at the wound, it must be elsewhere, perhaps somewhere less accessible. They're going to start a course of antibiotics and hope that does the trick.'

For the next couple of days, though we didn't dare to admit it, we were all aware that James's life hung in the balance. Then, miraculously, the antibiotics began to take effect and the spectre of another operation faded into the background. Once the change began, the speed of his recovery was unbelievable. For the rest of us, the sudden release from tension left emotions very much on the surface. We were irritable, excessively gay, and I, at least, prone to easy tears. He was going to be all right. He'd have to have a term off school, but by Christmas he should be back to normal. There was so much for which to be thankful.

On the Monday evening of Bank Holiday, we went out for a celebration dinner: Mother and Father, Cathy and Aunt Beth, Simon and I. The crisis had drawn us all together in a way that, left to itself, might have taken years. After the meal we drove Cathy and Aunt Beth home. Simon got out of the car with them and opened the gate. Cathy kissed me quickly, then turned to Simon.

'And if Cherry will allow me, I'd like to kiss you, for being such a tower of strength. Bless you, Simon.' She reached up and kissed him quickly, not as Rod had kissed me, on the cheek, but on the mouth. Perhaps it was my imagination, but it seemed that he was quieter than usual on the drive home.

The next day, exactly a week after our arrival, Simon and I set off south again.

'That's a week I shouldn't like to live through again,' he remarked feelingly as we turned once more onto the motorway.

'Amen to that.'

His hand left the wheel briefly to rest on my knee.

'You were a brick, Cherry. It couldn't have been easy. I was proud of you.'

His words were balm to my still smarting soul. 'There was so little I could do,' I said regretfully.

'You were *there*. Thank God you insisted on coming. All the time I was with Cathy I was on edge, trying not to let her see I was just as worried as she was. It was a hell of a strain. I don't know how many times I steadied myself just by remembering that you were there waiting for me.'

'Oh, Simon!' For the rest of the journey I sat in a daze of happiness. Simon had needed me, and I hadn't failed him after all.

Mrs. Charles awaited us with smiles and flowers. 'Oh sir, what a relief! I'm delighted the little lad's on the mend! What a time it must have been for—for his mother.' At least she had not said 'Mrs. Slade.'

She turned to me. 'By the way, madam, Mrs. Edwards phoned. When I told her what had happened she just sent her best wishes and didn't leave a message.'

'Thanks, Mrs. Charles, I'll ring her back later.'

Simon was sifting through the pile of letters which awaited him, but he looked up as I came into the room.

'Welcome home, darling! There's a drink waiting for you on the mantelpiece.'

As I went to get it I reflected with joy in my heart that it was the very first time he had called me 'darling.' At long last things had taken a decided turn for the better.

I phoned Helen later that evening and, in a mood of happy confidence, took the opportunity of issuing the rather overdue invitation to dinner.

I was glad to find that the prospect of entertaining the Edwardses no longer filled me with apprehension. The steady improvement in relations with Simon, begun up north, was giving me more security and therefore more self-confidence, and an incident during the dinner party served to pinpoint this.

It had been a hilarious evening and Tom, flushed with his third glass of wine, suddenly remarked, 'This reminds me of that hysterical meal we had at the Boat Club. Remember, Cherry?'

There was a small silence. I was aware that

Helen had kicked him under the table, and his kindly face reddened still more in confusion. I myself waited, tense, for the expected shaft of pain and when it failed to materialize, turned instinctively to Simon. He was watching me closely, and at the sight of my face he relaxed and his eyes lit up.

'Do afford me the courtesy of not mixing up my wives, old man!' he said lightly. 'Makes me feel like Henry VIII!'

The awkward moment passed in a gale of relieved laughter.

*　　　*　　　*

About a week later I was in the dining room removing dead flowers from a bowl when the telephone rang. Since Simon was up in the office I left him to answer it. Almost immediately I heard him come running down the stairs.

'Cherry? Are you there?'

'In the dining room.'

'That was the travel agent on the phone. They've managed to get us into a hotel despite the short notice. Cancellation, I believe.'

We hadn't discussed our approaching holiday in any depth and I was surprised he had made the arrangements without mentioning the fact.

'Good. Where are we going?'

'How does Majorca appeal?'

'Simon!' I gazed at him in delight, dripping water from the stems in my hand.

'I didn't want to mention it until it was confirmed in case the arrangements fell through, but I wanted something rather special for you, to make up for the last few months. It's a bit early to think in terms of a second honeymoon, but I'd like to feel we were starting again in some way, and I'll try not to make so many damn silly mistakes this time.'

He looked at me with a rueful smile. 'I'm not very good at saying what I feel, as you've noticed before, but perhaps you can manage to make something out of all that.'

'It'll do to begin with,' I said.

The next ten days passed swiftly. There were clothes to sort out and wash, airline tickets to be collected and lists to be made. One day an airmail letter arrived from Rod Cleveland, thanking us for our 'help and support.' He went on to say that Laurie was feeling much better and was convinced that all would be well 'next time.' If she was prepared to go through all that again, she must want a baby very much, I thought humbly.

When we landed, Majorca was bathed in warm sunshine. A taxi had been ordered by the hotel to meet us and I sat enthralled, staring out of the window at the wide sweep of Palma bay with its boats of all kinds; the new, concrete-faced hotels and discotheques; the pavements crowded with gaily dressed, tanned tourists. We left the centre of the town and the road began to climb, passing through the suburbs and then a string of small villages, before these too petered out as we approached the mountains. The road was steep and twisting and the taxi chugged painfully up it, rattling and bumping so much that Simon and I clung onto the edge of our seats. Tall trees crowded the sides of the road but breaks in them offered ever more majestic views falling away to the valleys below. Eventually, after about an hour, we reached the village where the hotel was situated. The hillsides, set back now from the road, were covered with olive trees and criss-crossed with irrigation channels, and at the side of the road some women of the village were doing their washing in a medieval-looking stone trough. The delightful old-world picture they made was, however, somewhat marred by the very modern boxes of detergent balanced precariously at their sides.

Simon and I were still laughing at this anachronism when the taxi drew up at the hotel. It was all that we'd hoped it would be, built like a traditional Majorcan house around a courtyard with an ancient date palm and a fountain in the centre. All the bedrooms led off this central court.

The swimming pool belonging to the hotel was down a little path between the olive groves, in a delightful setting of lemon trees and with a magnificent backdrop of mountains towering over it. This was the focal point for the hotel guests since the beach was a steep half hour's walk away. But Simon and I were not in the mood to be sociable. To everyone's surprise, we set off every morning provided with fruit, cold meat and cheese to save the necessity of returning for lunch, and spent an idyllic day in the privacy of the tiny bay which we had completely to ourselves.

'It's as well we at least have the exercise of getting here and back,' Simon remarked as we lay on the white sand. 'Otherwise all we should be doing is eating, sleeping, and a bit of unenergetic swimming. Not that I'm complaining.'

'I wish we could stay here forever,' I said dreamily.

He propped himself on one elbow and looked down at me. 'Happy, sweetheart? I seem to remember that last time I asked you that you were a bit evasive.'

'Well. I am now.'

His finger ran gently along the bridge of my nose. 'It hasn't been easy, has it? There were far more obstacles to overcome than I'd ever have believed, but we're on the right road now, aren't we?'

'Yes, I'm sure we are.'

The riot of yellow and orange which danced behind my eyelids darkened as his face came between me and the sun.

'I love you very much, my darling. Never forget that.'

At last! My arms flew around his neck and all the unhappiness of the past months disappeared in a delirium of joy and thankfulness.

Some time later, Simon remarked with satisfaction, 'Well, they can keep their swimming pool! Private beaches have a lot to recommend them!'

*   *   *

All too quickly the golden weeks sifted away like sand between our fingers. Sometimes in the evening we would walk down to the village and sit drinking coffee, trying to talk to the local people. Once we hired a car and spent a happy day exploring the mountain roads and surrounding villages.

'I don't want to go home,' I said sadly on our last evening, as we leaned on our balcony rail, gazing out at the grey-green slopes of olive trees. Back to Cathy's house, where we'd had so many tensions and misunderstandings.

'I think the truth of the matter,' Simon said slowly, 'is that it doesn't feel like home to you, does it? You tried to tell me that at the beginning, but I thought you'd grow into it. I think I've known for some time that you weren't going to.'

'I have tried,' I said, 'but it still feels like

another woman's house to me. And not just any woman, either, but your wife. Even Mrs. Charles adds to the impression. I resent her and she resents me. She still insists on arranging ornaments in a certain way—probably Cathy's way—even though I've repeatedly asked her not to, and I rearrange them every time she dusts. It's such a stupid little thing, but it's as though she's trying to show me it isn't really my house. And it's also knowing that you and Cathy chose all the carpets and furnishings together. I feel like an intruder, somehow.'

'I didn't realize it went as deep as that, darling, I'm sorry. It was very thoughtless of me not to have realized how you'd feel. But these last few weeks, an idea's been growing in my mind of selling up altogether and starting again from scratch—not taking so much as a stick of furniture with us. Part of the fresh start. Does that appeal to you?'

'But Simon, wouldn't you mind?'

'Not in the slightest. As a matter of fact, I was talking to Rod about it. A friend of his is coming over to England shortly on a five-year contract. He'd asked Rod to keep an eye open for a suitable house, furnished or unfurnished. That might be just the answer.'

'To buy or to rent?'

'It would depend on how they liked it. It would probably be cheaper for them to buy it in the long run, since it will appreciate in value. So, Mrs. Slade, what do you fancy? A modern house, a country cottage, a flat in town?'

'Oh, I don't know.' I felt excitement move in me. 'I'll have to think about it. Nothing too big, though.' I was thinking of all those empty bedrooms. 'Just big enough for the two of us.'

I felt his momentary stillness, but all he said was, 'Tom's in the property market. We'll have a word with him when we get back, and I'll drop a line to Rod too. Now, will that make leaving Majorca any easier?'

'Oh yes, darling! And thank you!"

'So we'll find us a house, and settle down, and live happily ever after. Right?'

'Yes, please,' I said.

CHAPTER ELEVEN

So we flew home from Majorca, and for the first time I was able to enter that house without the faint sense of misgiving which had always disturbed me. Simon broke the news to Mrs. Charles that we would be moving as soon as we could find somewhere suitable, and he also told her of the possibility of the Americans coming.

'They might be glad for you to stay on, or for John to continue seeing to the garden. If the deal goes through, I'll mention it if you like.'

She seemed neither surprised nor perturbed. She had probably guessed, that I wouldn't stay long in Cathy's house. Meanwhile, the post brought exciting details of houses which might interest us, and I spent long hours poring over them.

At the weekends, we would set out full of hope to view the selected properties, only to learn with dismay that we seldom saw eye to eye with the estate agents over descriptions or amenities, and our initial expectations of finding somewhere reasonably quickly began to fade.

In mid-October Simon was able to return to work in the newly acquired office buildings and the guest room was restored to its *status quo*. I wasn't sorry. Its conversion had held too many painful memories. We received a letter from Ed Parry, Rod's friend, saying that Rod's description of the house interested them very much. They would be flying to England after the New Year and were prepared to pay a deposit on the house, to hold it pending their arrival.

'Mother, father and four children,' Simon remarked. 'Nice to think of it being a full house again. Well, my love, we'd better hurry up and find somewhere or we'll be out on the streets! Tom was saying something about an estate of new houses which might be of interest, but they're not completed yet. We could have a look at the show house, though.'

I wasn't sure I liked the thought of a brand-new house with the attendant wilderness of unmade garden that would go with it. But as Simon said, time was passing and so far my dream house had failed to materialize. And when it did, we almost missed it.

We had gone, despite my reluctance, to look at Tom's new estate, and had spent an exhausting afternoon climbing up and down ladders where staircases would eventually be, straddling joists and trying to imagine how the finished house would look. Thick mud was everywhere and, despite my care, my shoes were caked with it. Admittedly, the show house was impressive. It even had turf laid in the garden and a prefabricated goldfish pond, but somehow it failed to interest me.

'We could go along with any of the ideas of decorating and furnishing that appeal to us,' Simon reminded me. 'Unlike most people, we don't have to consider what we already have. They've got some rather good touches here and there.'

'I don't know—' I stood undecided, unable to pinpoint my objections. 'It hasn't any character,' I said finally.

'All the better, we can stamp it with our own!'

'Oh Simon, I really don't know. I'm probably past being able to make a decision. We've seen so many, but—'

'If you're even remotely interested we'd

better at least put a deposit on it. They're being snapped up pretty quickly, and a deposit doesn't commit us to anything.'

'All right. I certainly like the nearby village, and according to the particulars there's a fast train service to London.'

While Simon wrote a cheque for the deposit, I lowered myself gingerly onto one of the elegant brocade-seated dining chairs. I was tired and frustrated. I hadn't realized how exhausting house hunting could be, or how disillusioning. At least now we had the possibility of a home which, on the face of it, had a great deal to recommend it. I should have been jubilant, but instead I was fighting back tears of disappointment.

'Come on sweetheart, you're tired out. Home now, for a cup of tea and a lazy evening.'

Reluctantly I stood up, my muddy shoes still dangling from my hand. 'How long will it take us to get home?'

'Only about half an hour.'

'So if we did live here we needn't lose touch with Sally and Sylvia and the others.' There was a grain of comfort in that.

We threaded our way cautiously over planks laid across the most treacherous puddles and got into the car. I turned back to look at the site and the skeletal houses marooned among the mud and puddles brought a wave of desolation. Of course, it would be completely different when people were actually living there. People? Or us?

We drove back down the sloping road and through the little village we had passed before. It was in two distinct halves separated by the railway line: New Woodend through which we had just come, with modern banks, launderettes and supermarkets—and Old Woodend, over the bridge we were now crossing, with antique shops, Elizabethan-style coffee houses and luscious homemade pastry shops.

'I do like this village,' I said again. 'It has the best of two worlds.' My eyes scanned the narrow pavements as we came to the end of the village street and the road veered away to the right. 'Just a minute, Simon—can you stop?'

'What's the matter? Have you left something behind?'

'No, look—over there to the left. A "For Sale" notice!'

'Look, darling, we've just put a deposit—'

'Please! Please let's just look!'

With a muttered comment to the detriment of women, Simon reversed slowly and stopped opposite the sign I had seen.

'We can't see anything over this hedge!'

'The entrance must be down that little side road.'

Simon glanced at his watch. 'Look, Cherry, do you really think it's worth it? Surely we've had enough for one day, and time's getting on.'

'Please!' I begged. He sighed and turned the car into the side road. A few yards along, we came to a white five-bar gate. Simon stopped and we sat staring up the cobbled path at a delightful old house which stood demurely at the end of it.

'"Briar Cottage,"' I read. 'I wonder if they'd mind us looking round. It feels like home, even from here!'

'Are you serious?'

'I've never been more so. Please, darling.'

Together we went up the path. Within the loving circle of the high hedge lay a charming old-world garden, complete with sundial and herbacious borders. Now, in the fading light of the October afternoon, dahlias and chrysanthemums lit the shadows with splashes of colour. The front door was set in a deep recess and there was a wooden bench on either side of the tiled porch. Simon pressed the bell and a young woman came to open the door.

'I'm sorry to disturb you,' he began. 'I know we haven't an appointment, but if it isn't too inconvenient we'd very much like to see over the house.'

'Well—yes, all right, come in. We were just going to have tea. Perhaps you'd like a cup?'

'If it's no trouble, we certainly would.'

The hall was square, with the staircase protected by beautifully carved bannisters. She said, 'Would you mind coming into the kitchen? The children are still at the messy stage and we usually eat in there.'

She opened a door at the back of the hall. 'Some people to see the house, dear.' She turned to us. 'I didn't ask your name?'

'Slade,' Simon supplied.

'Ours is Franklyn.'

Her husband came forward to meet us. 'I'm afraid we're not very spick and span, but at least you'll see how it looks under normal conditions. Do sit down. Get on with your sandwiches, children.'

Two round pairs of eyes were staring at us.

'It's a perfect house for children,' Mrs. Franklyn said. 'The garden's so safe, and there's an old barn at the back which we've converted into a playroom. Have you any yourselves?'

'No,' I said.

'Well, of course it could be used for anything—a studio, or study, even a spare bedroom because there's a little cloakroom over there too.'

I was trying to listen to her, but I was watching Simon's face as he bent down to talk to the children, and there was a burning sensation at the base of my throat.

'Actually,' I amended, 'I should have said I've none of my own. I have three stepchildren who come to stay. I'm sure they'd love it.'

'There are apple trees to climb, and a swing

hanging from one of them. I'm afraid you won't be able to see much of the garden at the moment. It's getting dark so early now, isn't it?'

I sat back and looked round the large friendly room. Mrs. Franklyn went on, 'My husband's an architect and he was very careful that we should modernize discreetly. We have all modern conveniences of course, but I think we've managed to stop them intruding on the overall atmosphere.'

'Is anyone else interested in it?' I asked fearfully.

'Yes, a few people are, but nothing's been settled.' She smiled suddenly. 'As a matter of fact Dennis is losing patience with me, but I don't want to sell the house to just *anyone*. It must be someone who'd love it as much as we do.'

'We would,' I said.

She looked at me consideringly. 'Yes, I think you would. But you've not seen much of it yet, you'd better reserve judgment.'

'I knew when we stopped at the gate.'

'How odd, so did I when we bought it. It'll break our hearts to leave it, but my husband's firm has moved him up north. There's nothing else we can do.'

Mr. Franklyn, who had been talking to Simon, came over to us. 'If you've finished your tea, Mrs. Slade, shall we start the tour? We'll begin with a quick look at the garden before the light fades any more.'

We went out of the back door and Mrs. Franklyn drew back the kitchen curtains to let the light flood across the lawn. The barn was over to the right, just one large room, at the moment strewn with toys, with windows along one wall and a radiator to warm it.

'There's a loo and washbasin in there.' Mr. Franklyn pointed to a door. 'Otherwise, this is all there is. We'd thought at one time of dividing it but never got round to it. At the bottom of the garden, which you can barely see now, there are about a dozen fruit trees— apple, pear, Victoria plum. Joyce is inordinately proud of the fact that we once had peaches growing against the back of the house. It faces south, and as you can see, is very sheltered.'

Mrs. Franklyn was still supervising the children's tea as her husband showed Simon the workings of the central heating boiler.

'Right, now we'll move on into the sitting room. There were two smallish rooms here, which we decided to knock into one. We're rather pleased with the effect.'

It was certainly a charming room, long and low-ceilinged with French windows opening onto the little patio at the back of the house.

'We're sideways onto the main road, but the hedge keeps out most of the traffic noise. It's not very busy anyway, since they built the bypass. If you look up just here you can see from the beams how the rooms were divided. And the window embrasure will give you an idea of the thickness of the walls. Solid stone, and as snug and watertight as you could wish.'

As we followed him across the hall to the dining room, I gripped Simon's hand tightly. His eyes were shining and he seemed as excited as I was.

'This is only small, as you see. I took the fireplace out to make more room—it wasn't particularly beautiful anyway. Nothing like the one in the sitting room, which we've made a feature of. We seldom have an open fire, but when we do we burn apple logs and they smell glorious. And that's all downstairs, except a minute cloakroom next to the kitchen. We converted it from the original pantry.'

As we went up the stairs I trailed my hand lovingly along the polished wood of the old bannisters. They felt smooth and cool. There were three bedrooms; the fourth had been turned into an extra bathroom. They were all of medium size, and would certainly allow us to accommodate the children when they visited us.

'And that,' Mr. Franklyn concluded, 'is the lot. What do you think of it?'

Simon put an arm round my shoulders. 'If you look at my wife's face I think you'll have your answer.'

'That's how I hoped you'd feel. My wife had preconceived ideas about who she'd sell to, which I might tell you has caused some awkward moments. But you, praise be, apparently fill the bill! If you want it, it's yours.'

I held my breath.

'We want it,' said Simon.

*   *   *

Everything happened very quickly after that. The Franklyns were eager to be out as soon as possible. He was already working in Cumbria and only able to get home at the weekends. By our second visit we were on first name terms. Since Dennis was an architect, he was able to provide us with accurate measurements of the rooms, and Simon and I embarked on the exhilarating business of choosing furniture.

'They're asking quite a hefty price, you know,' he reminded me. 'Until we know for certain that the Americans will agree with the valuers' price on the other house and contents, we'll have to go carefully.'

'Then let's furnish it slowly with what we really want, instead of trying to do everything at once. It must be just right.'

As though to make up for what had gone before, things now started to go our way. We found exactly the dining suite we were looking for, material for the curtains which matched the chair seats to perfection, a beautiful old oak chest to do duty as a hall table. I drove myself mercilessly to track down just the shade of carpet I wanted for the bedroom, and persuaded Simon to drive miles to auctions and sales of antique furniture.

The weekend before they moved out, the Franklyns invited us to their farewell party, to meet the neighbours. Everyone seemed very friendly—and, I thought happily, they were meeting Simon and myself together, as a pair. There was no one here to compare, to think back to when there had been someone else in my place.

It was hot and noisy in the long low room and I remembered Sally's party, when I had escaped to sit talking with Jeremy in the kitchen. I decided to do the same again. My legs were aching and I wanted to relax for a few minutes.

I stood for a while in the hall, the noise of the party muffled behind the closed door. My eyes lingered lovingly on the ornate brass doorknobs, the solid oak of the front door, the graceful sweep of the staircase. Our house, mine and Simon's. Soon it would be completely ours.

Dennis came out of the kitchen with a jug of ice. 'Hello, getting the feel of the place?'

'Just having a breather.'

'Well, feel free to wander. All I ask is, don't wake the kids! It's a miracle to me they're sleeping through this lot as it is!' He disappeared back into the melee and the door closed behind him.

Feeling rather diffident despite his permission, I went upstairs. In the main bedroom I stopped to repair my make-up, seeing the room not so much as it was now, with the depressing packing cases already stacked in one corner, but as it would be, with Simon's dressing gown behind the door and the soft blue carpet under my feet.

One of the children gave a little cry in its sleep. I waited to see if it would wake, but all was quiet. I hesitated outside their door and then peeped inside. Penny, the four-year-old, lay spread across the bed, her arms above her head. A lovely house for children. Although Joyce had given no hint of it, I knew that was the only respect in which we had disappointed her. She had wanted to think of other children sleeping where hers did now, playing in their lovely spacious barn.

With a sigh I made my way down to the homely peace of the kitchen. Here I'd sit with a cup of coffee when Simon had left for work in the mornings. And I'd be in here listening for the sound of his car while I prepared the evening meal. I shouldn't have to share the care of the house with any Mrs. Charles. There would simply be Simon and me. The children would come, of course, I told myself, to still the recurring twinge of conscience. James's illness had drawn us together and from now on we would be happy together. But that would have to be enough. I pushed away the memory of baby Charlotte, as I was increasingly having to do these days, and as always there was an underlying sense of loss. But I couldn't risk it. If Simon had to go back to Africa at any time, I must be free to go with him.

The door opened and Joyce came in. 'Hello, I thought I'd find you here! I slip away myself from time to time, to recharge my batteries. You look tired—are you all right?'

'We've been having a fairly hectic time lately, dashing around the showrooms and everything, and when I get to bed I'm overtired and don't sleep too well.'

'When do you think you'll be moving in?'

'We hope to be here for Christmas. There's some decorating we want to do and a six-week delivery on some of the furniture, but the American family will be over early in January.'

'It's lovely here at Christmas,' Joyce said wistfully, 'especially if it snows. In fact, it's lovely all the year round: spring blossoms, summer flowers, autumn fruits and leaves. You name it, we've got it—in abundance! Or rather, you have.'

'I hope you won't miss it too much.'

'I shall, of course. But Dennis has found something he thinks will suit us, so our furniture won't have to be in storage for very long. Are you sure you're all right, Cherry?'

A hot wave of weakness had flooded over me, leaving me shaken and breathless. 'Yes thanks. As I said, I've been rather overdoing it, that's all.'

She looked at me searchingly, then gave a little smile. 'Suit yourself!'

Was it my imagination, or was the room suddenly unbearably hot? I looked up at her and her image seemed to shimmer like a mirage.

'What do you mean?'

'Oh come now, if you want to keep it a secret, fair enough. But at least give me credit for having eyes in my head!'

The meaning of her words soaked slowly through the cotton wool in my head.

'No!' I said violently. 'No, you're wrong.'

'If you say so. But don't forget I've had two myself. I'd be very surprised if—Cherry! Oh I'm sorry, I didn't mean to upset you.'

Tears were cascading down my face like a broken dam. 'Whatever's the matter? Don't you *want* a baby?'

'No, no I don't!' I sobbed wildly. 'I don't want to share Simon with anyone!'

'You don't have to share what is part of yourself,' she said gently. 'Do stop crying, it can't be good for you—' *in your condition.* She bit off the words but I knew what she meant and cried all the harder. Oddly enough, it didn't occur to me to doubt her diagnosis. As soon as she'd spoken, I'd recognized it for the truth.

'Look,' she said helplessly, 'a baby would be half you and half Simon. Isn't that the most wonderful thing you can think of?'

It was useless to attempt to explain, to tell her that only now, for the first time, was I sure of his love and that, selfishly, I wasn't prepared to relinquish any part of it.

'He already has three children,' I said a little more calmly. 'That should be enough, surely.'

'Well, of course you know how he feels about it and it's no business of mine. I'm just sorry that I upset you like this, and of course, I could be wrong. It may well be that you've simply been overdoing things, as you said. Once the upheaval's over—and it won't be long now—you can settle down and relax. Just you and Simon.' Her eyes rested for a second on the highchair in the corner. 'But in my opinion you'll be missing an awful lot.'

Rather shamefacedly I tried to apologize for my breakdown, but she brushed it aside.

'Forget it. The tears will have helped to ease the tension.'

But I was not deceived by her recantation, and going home in the car I tried to remember dates which had come and gone without my realizing it. And what they portended seemed—to be the most cruel blow of all.

CHAPTER TWELVE

The next morning I was still weak and exhausted. Simon looked at me in concern. 'There's no need for you to get up, darling. Have a morning in bed, you've earned it. You've been doing far too much, you know. You'll need to get your strength back before the actual move.'

'Perhaps you're right. I'll stay here for a while, anyway,' I said listlessly.

'You're not ill, are you?' Anxiety sharpened his voice.

'No, only tired.'

But no sooner had he gone downstairs—than I had to make a dash for the bathroom. Afterwards, sick and shivering, I crept back to bed and buried my face in the pillow.

By the time Sally called round later that morning, I had managed to dress and stagger downstairs.

'There's some Georgian silver being auctioned over at Richmond,' she told me. 'I was wondering if you'd like me to run you over, but you don't look very good this morning.'

'Oh, I'm all right,' I answered brightly—and indeed, after a cup of tea and some dry toast, I did feel better. 'We were at a party last night—it's probably a hangover!'

'Knowing the amount you drink, I doubt that! Perhaps you ate something that disagreed with you.'

'Perhaps. Anyway, I'd like to go, Sally. Thanks for thinking of me.'

'If I can find something reasonable, I might be tempted myself. Christmas is coming, after all.'

So we set off on another long drive, another snatched lunch, another afternoon walking and standing and waiting about. And I bought a pair of candelabra.

'You won't have Mrs. Charles to polish those for you, remember!' Sally said, looking at the intricate scrolls rather dubiously.

'Believe me, I shall enjoy looking after everything at Briar Cottage all by myself!'

'I'm longing to see it—it sounds gorgeous.'

'You'll be one of our first visitors, I promise!'

Back home, I collapsed into a chair and put my feet up. I was sound asleep when Simon came in.

'Still not too good? I hope you had a quiet day?'

My mouth twitched. 'Not exactly. Sally drove me over to a sale at Richmond. What do you think of the candelabra?' I nodded over to where they glinted in the firelight.

'They look great, but you really shouldn't have gone out today, you know. No wonder you're worn out. Don't dare stir out of this house tomorrow on any account!'

'But I must. I'm coming into London with you, remember? There's that material I want to look at and I've arranged to meet the girls for lunch.'

'Look, Cherry, you must be sensible about this. You have to draw the line somewhere.'

'I'll be all right after a good night's sleep. Don't worry.'

Much against his will, Simon complied with my request for a lift into town the next morning. I felt a little better and was trying to convince myself that the whole scare had been a false alarm, but Sue and Lucy did nothing to reassure me.

'Now, what's this news you have for us?' Lucy inquired. 'As if I didn't know!'

'I don't see how you can,' I said quickly. 'It's that Simon and I have bought the most heavenly cottage, and we're pulling out all the stops to be in by Christmas.'

'Well, that wasn't what I was expecting but it sounds very exciting. What was wrong with the house you have now?'

'It was Cathy's,' I said.

'And that's all you have to tell us?' prompted Sue.

'Isn't it enough? It is for me, I assure you! Every second seems to be spent in planning and making lists and measuring things.'

The waiter came over with the menu and we studied it together.

'*Blanquette de veau* for me,' Lucy said at once. 'That's a favourite of yours too, isn't it, Cherry?'

But the thought of the rich, thick sauce made me feel queasy. 'I—think I'll just have fish today,' I said carefully, and, catching their quickly exchanged glances, added hastily, 'I've had an upset stomach the last couple of days.'

They didn't probe any further and started asking about the cottage, which I was only too ready to talk about. We parted, promising to be in touch again soon.

For the second consecutive day, I was asleep when Simon came home.

'Cherry, I want you to go along and see Jeremy. You're not at all yourself at the moment. Perhaps he can prescribe something to put you back on your feet.'

My fingers gripped the arms of my chair. 'There's no need for that. I'll get a bottle of tonic next time I'm at the chemist.'

'No. I'd rather you saw Jeremy. I want to know exactly what's wrong.'

But once I saw Jeremy, my fragile self-deception would be abruptly ended.

'Tomorrow,' Simon added firmly.

Perhaps, after all, it would be a relief to know definitely, one way or the other.

*   *   *

'Well, Cherry!' Jeremy smiled kindly at me

across his desk. 'Not much doubt about that, I'd say. You're roughly seven weeks pregnant, which makes the big day—let's see—sometime in July. We can work it out more exactly if you've got a note of—'

He broke off. The great, betraying tears had started again. There was to be no reprieve. Simon and I wouldn't have our new home to ourselves after all.

'You mustn't worry, you know. Just try to ease up on things. Simon tells me you've been trying to do too much. I don't think he suspected this, though. Haven't you said anything to him?'

I shook my head. 'I hoped it wasn't true. Jeremy, no one seems to believe me when I say so, but I don't *want* a baby!'

His face was grave. 'I'm sorry to hear that, but try not to worry too much. I'm quite sure when it arrives you won't want to send it back!' When I didn't smile, he added quietly, 'There's nothing to be afraid of, you know.'

'But there is,' I answered in a low voice. 'Look what happened to Cathy and Simon once the babies came. They were only happy for the first year.'

Jeremy leaned back in his chair and let his breath out in a long sigh. 'I see!'

'I'm glad you understand, because no one else does. Things haven't been easy for Simon and me, for various reasons. We've only just come really together and I don't want anything—anything at all—to spoil it.'

'But a baby won't spoil it. It'll make your happiness complete. Look, Cherry, forget about Cathy. The problem there was almost exactly the reverse of yours. You're afraid of sharing Simon's love with the baby, whereas she seemed afraid of sharing the children's love with him. If you want my advice, tell Simon about the baby straight away and let him share in every aspect of preparing for it, even of caring for it later, if he wants to. Don't shut him out. He missed out on a great deal with the others.'

He stood up. 'Come and see me again in a month's time. I'm sure you'll feel very differently by then. I'm giving you a prescription for iron pills. They'll help, but you must slacken the pace a little. Now, try to look a little more cheerful, or you'll frighten the patients in the waiting room!'

His hand under my elbow guided me to the door, and I was through the waiting room and on the pavement outside. Mechanically, I started to walk.

'Mrs. Slade!'

I turned as a girl pushing a pram came hurrying towards me. It was Angela Davies—and Charlotte, unrecognizable now, rosy and round-cheeked banging on the pram cover with a wooden spoon.

'She's certainly grown since I last saw her!' I said with an effort.

'Well, she's five and a half months now. I hear you're moving?'

'Yes, in about a fortnight.'

'Sally was saying you're not going very far, so we may see you again. I hope you'll be very happy in your new home.'

I stood looking after them, remembering the strange sensations I'd felt bending over Charlotte's cot last summer. Perhaps, after all, everything would be all right. Perhaps I'd been putting importance on the wrong things. For the first time I thought of the coming child as a personality in its own right, and experienced a lift of excited anticipation.

I walked on slowly, hardly knowing where I was going, my mind whirling, adjusting, acclimatizing. On an impulse, I crossed the road and went into the babywear shop. What I needed, I thought, was something concrete, a sign of my acceptance. A pair of minute white bootees stood on the counter. Could any foot be small enough to fit into them?

'I'll have these,' I said. I didn't look at the assistant, nor did I wait for her to wrap them. I put the exact money down on the counter, stuffed the tiny things deep in my coat pocket, and left hurriedly, no doubt leaving her staring after me.

How could I tell Simon? I must choose the right moment, say exactly the right thing, or everything could still be threatened.

'What did Jeremy say?' he asked as soon as

he came home, but before I could reply Mrs. Charles came to the door with a query about dinner, and somehow the moment was lost.

'Well?' he prompted when she'd gone.

My courage evaporated. 'He gave me some iron pills. There's nothing—wrong.' Medically at least, that was true.

'Well, that's a relief. All the same, take things easy for the rest of the week, and then on Saturday we can go over and see how things are going at the cottage.'

'All right,' I agreed. Later, I told myself, after dinner. I'll tell him after dinner, as soon as the right moment comes.

*   *   *

It was Saturday and we were at the cottage, and I still hadn't told Simon the news. The longer I delayed, the harder it became to broach the subject. I was over my morning sickness, if that was what it had been, and the few days' rest had made me feel well again. Could Jeremy possibly have been mistaken?

It was strange to be there without the Franklyns. The place had a bewildered air, with its uncarpeted boards and echoing rooms. It seemed to be in a kind of limbo, between one existence and another. Much, in fact, as I felt myself to be.

'Cherry, come here!'

I went to the dining room to join Simon.

'Look, the undercoat's on, It looks great! doesn't it? Can you picture the suite in here, and the curtains? Not to mention the candelabra! Incredible to think we'll actually be living here in a couple of weeks! The decorators should have finished by Friday, so next weekend we can clean everything out, ready for the men to come and lay the carpets. Once they're down, all the stuff that's ready can be delivered.'

He moved to the window. 'That spire over there must be the church in the village. It's a good flat lawn round at the side here. We can set out the croquet when the children come. Let's go and look at the sitting room.'

He caught my hand and led me across the hall. 'The sage green carpet was an inspiration for here. Clever little thing, aren't you, with a natural eye for colour!'

I tried to match his mood but not very successfully, and he glanced at my face. 'You're a bit pale, love, despite those damned pills. Sit down and rest for a moment. There's only the windowsill, but at least it's quite wide!'

I lowered myself carefully onto the sill. The glass struck cold at my back. 'Have you any regrets, Simon, to be leaving Cheston?'

'None at all. As you said, this felt like home straight away. I should never have expected you to live in Cathy's house, but time was the main factor. I wanted to get you married as soon as possible, in case you changed your mind!'

I looked up at him in surprise. 'Did you think I might?'

'Of course I did—I was terrified! I had to talk you into it in the first place, and I was convinced that David bloke would show up again and you'd go off with him after all!'

I said slowly, 'You didn't exactly sweep me off my feet with protestations of undying love!'

'No, I rather overdid the reasoned approach, didn't I? It was double indemnity, really, partly to protect myself in case you rejected me, and partly fear of frightening you off before you were ready to love me. And let's face it, darling, it took you long enough to get round to it!'

Had he really thought that? The time for a full confession was long overdue. I drew a deep breath.

'As a matter of fact, Mr. Slade, you entirely misread the situation. I've loved you from the first moment I saw you—in Yorkshire, not in London.'

He stared at me. 'I don't understand.'

'I fell for you hook, line and sinker when you married Cathy. As I grew older, I used to measure all my boy friends against you, but they never came up to scratch!'

He said unsteadily, 'But my darling girl, the first time I asked you to marry me, you turned me down!'

'Because you so obviously didn't love me,' I said in a low voice, and at his violent movement, added quickly, 'You must admit that was how it seemed. At first I didn't think I could bear it, but then I realized it was better than nothing.'

'But darling, if only I'd known! What a lot of time we wasted!'

'There seemed to be so much against me: the house, Cathy and the children, even Rona. You seemed to care for all of them more than you did for me.'

'Darling, no!' His voice was anguished but now that I'd started I had to go on, so that it could all be forgotten once and for all.

'There was always something between us, some barrier you put up to stop me getting too close. It didn't really start to go until James's illness.' I looked up at him. 'Do you realize that when you told me you loved me, that day on the beach, it was the very first time?'

'It was the first time I felt sure enough of you to say it aloud. Several times I came very close to it but something always held me back. Fear of committing myself, I suppose. A legacy from last time. Thank heaven we've got it all cleared up at last.' He shivered. 'God, it's cold! What a time to embark on confessions! Let's go and warm ourselves up with a cup of tea in the village café.'

'Just a moment, Simon. Since we're on the truth game, I've one more confession.'

He looked at me quickly. 'What is it?'

I felt in my coat pocket. The bootees were still there. Slowly I drew them out and held them on the palm of my hand. There was a timeless silence. Slowly, almost painfully, his eyes came to my face, questioning, wild hope beginning to dawn.

I forced my stiff lips into a smile. 'That was the full diagnosis—the reason for the iron pills.'

His face blazed with such joy that I couldn't look at him. 'Darling, you're sure? Jeremy really confirmed it?'

I nodded, quite unable to speak, and he sobered slightly. 'But I thought you—'

'Let's say it wasn't exactly planned.'

'But you're glad now, aren't you?'

To save my life I couldn't have denied him that moment.

'Of course,' I said steadily. I went on, putting my fear into the past tense for his benefit. 'What I was so afraid of was that things might start to go wrong for us, like when James was born. And they've only just started to go right.'

Despite myself, my lip trembled. He gave an exclamation, and pulled me up and into his arms. 'Was that why you didn't want a baby? Oh darling, why didn't you tell me? I could have explained.'

'Explained what?'

'How it was with Cathy. I suppose there are

women who only want to be wives—I was afraid you might be one—but there are others who only want to be mothers, and Cathy was one of them. A husband was simply a means to an end. All she really wanted was children. You can imagine what that did to my self-esteem.'

'Oh darling, she loved you!' How could she have helped it?

'Not really.' The remembered bitterness was momentarily back in his voice. 'You know, I'd never intended to discuss this with anyone, ever. It seems a little disloyal, but I have a loyalty to you too, and if I'd been more open about it I could have saved you a lot of unhappiness. Anyway, the fact was that she seemed almost to resent any sign of affection those children showed me. She had to come first with them. I don't think it was entirely her fault. It probably stemmed from the way she was brought up, never knowing her father. You know how close she is to Beth. For eighteen years, those two were everything to each other. There were no men in Cathy's childhood—except your father, of course—and her mother was her whole universe. She wanted to mean as much to her own children: an ideal, self-sufficient mother.' He gave a twisted smile. 'Did you know I have a degree in psychology?'

I said slowly, 'I suppose that could be the explanation.'

'I'm sure it is. It hurt like hell, of course. She

213

was all mother, and hardly wife at all. The children always came first, in everything. That's a hard pill for any man to swallow.'

I pressed against him. 'You'll always come first with me, darling, however many children we have. And I'll need all the help I can get. I don't know a thing about babies!' I thought again of Charlotte, but for the first time with unclouded happiness.

For a while we stood close together, not speaking, busy with our own thoughts. Then he said softly, 'You know I'm glad we got it all sorted out here. It's a wonderful memory to start building on.'

'Actually, I have an earlier one. It was here, at the party, that Joyce first hinted what might be the reason for my tiredness. It had never occurred to me.'

'And you kept it quiet all this time?'

'I had to be sure, of you as well as the baby.'

He looked down into my face. 'And now you are?'

I drew a breath of pure happiness. 'Yes, darling, now I really am.'

We hope you have enjoyed this Large Print book. Other Chivers Press or Thorndike Press Large Print books are available at your library or directly from the publishers.

For more information about current and forthcoming titles, please call or write, without obligation, to:

Chivers Large Print
published by BBC Audiobooks Ltd
St James House, The Square
Lower Bristol Road
Bath BA2 3SB
UK
email: bbcaudiobooks@bbc.co.uk
www.bbcaudiobooks.co.uk

OR

Thorndike Press
295 Kennedy Memorial Drive
Waterville
Maine 04901
USA
www.gale.com/thorndike
www.gale.com/wheeler

All our Large Print titles are designed for easy reading, and all our books are made to last.